HIGHER,
FURTHER,
FASTER

HIGHER,
FURTHER,
FASTER

HIGHER, FURTHER, FASTER

LIZA PALMER

centum

MARVEL CAPTAIN MARVEL: HIGHER, FURTHER, FASTER

A CENTUM BOOK 978-1-913265-45-8

Published in Great Britain by Centum Books Ltd

This edition published 2019

1 3 5 7 9 10 8 6 4 2

© 2019 MARVEL

Centum Books Ltd, 20 Devon Square, Newton Abbot, Devon, TQ12 2HR, UK.

Books@centumbooksltd.co.uk

CENTUM BOOKS Limited Reg. No. 07641486

A CIP catalogue record for this book is available from the British Library.

Printed in United Kingdom

CHAPTER 1

"IT'S LIKE YOU'RE NOT EVEN TRYING," I TAUNT.
The deep rumble rips through the sky. It's getting closer.

"You can't hide from me." I squeeze my eyes closed. "I'd know you anywhere."

The thundering engine roars in reply and shakes the ground as it closes in.

"I've got you," I say, smiling. The hairs on the back of my neck stand on end as its effortless growl draws near. Closer. Closer. Closer. And just as it's overhead, I yell—

"The P-Fifty-One-D Mustang!" I open my eyes just as the pilot lines up the plane with the runway.

"I knew it!" I shout triumphantly to the sky.

Sitting back on the hood of my car, I watch as the pilot deftly lands the P-51D Mustang plane at a nearby airport, the screech of wheels signaling that both vehicle and pilot are safe and sound. The sky grows quiet once more.

With a sigh, I open my ancient canteen and sip the still-too-hot tea. I can feel its warmth traveling down my throat. I tear off the last bit of toast and jam that bravely survived the hours-long road trip, and pull my plaid blanket tight around me. Where I come from, it's usually more than enough to ward off the earliest of daylight chills, but today, even all bundled up, I realize this colder Colorado weather is going to be something to get used to.

And then . . . I can feel it in my chest before I even hear it. Another magnificent rumble amidst the far-off clouds.

I close my eyes, lift my face upward, and listen. I've always been happiest sitting on the hood of my car with this same plaid blanket, canteen full of hot tea, and bread and jam, listening to planes take off and land. The scenery around me might be different now, but the game is intuitive no matter the surroundings—these sounds are seared deep into my bones, as familiar as a favorite song.

"Piper Saratoga," I reverently whisper. I open my eyes just as the little plane soars overhead and smile as I am, once again, correct.

I check my watch. I'm still early. Way too early. But I can't wait anymore. I've been waiting my whole life. And now that the day is finally here, I can no longer contain myself.

Today still doesn't feel real.

A dream I once had turned into a fantasy I dared not mention aloud. But then with every step, every checked box, every application, every essay, every letter of recommendation, every physical test, and every envelope that came in the mail, I held my breath as I waited to see if I really would get the opportunity to become the person I'd always imagined.

And then the letter came. And the letter became a promise. And that promise became a red-circled day on my calendar. And then that red-circled day became a packing list, and then that packing list became a messy pile on my bed that definitely was never going to fit into any duffle bag. And then that duffle bag got loaded into my gassed-up Mustang. And then that gassed-up

Mustang drove away from the hometown I always knew wouldn't be able to keep me forever.

And now, that gassed-up Mustang is parked just outside this small airport in Colorado so I can feel like me again in these unreal hours before that long-ago dream finally becomes a reality.

I start at the United States Air Force Academy today. I am finally going to fly.

I'm going to spend the next four years making sure I become the very best airman I can be. Airman Danvers. Airman First Class Danvers. How about Master Sergeant Carol Danvers. Or even Second Lieutenant Danvers. No . . . what about:

Captain Carol Danvers—the first female fighter pilot in the Air Force.

A puff of excited breath bursts out into the cold morning air. I can't stall any longer. I screw on the top of my canteen as tightly as I can. I ball up the napkin I had wrapped my toast and jam in, and slide down the hood of my car as gently as possible. I creak open the trunk of my Mustang and place the now-folded plaid blanket inside, along with the canteen and balled-up napkin. I shift my duffle bag and find that I'm fidgeting and nervous as I arrange and rearrange the trunk's contents. I want to get there and not get there all at the same time.

It's almost like I don't want to wake from my lifelong dream only to realize that I can't—

No.

I was born to fly.

Of all the things I've ever doubted, that was never one of them.

Filled with a reinforced sense of determination, I slam the trunk closed.

As I walk around to the driver's-side door, I can feel another overhead plane's low growl in the pit of my stomach. I curl my fingers around the Mustang's door handle. The engine's singsongy hum thrills me as the plane makes its approach. This one growls and purrs at the same time. It's both magnetic and menacing. And it's more beautiful than anything I've ever heard.

I screw my eyes shut and pay attention, unable to resist one last turn. It's not a Cessna. Of course not. It's not a newer plane either, so that'd rule out all the Beechcrafts. Is it a Marchetti? No. That's . . . It could be an old Ryan PT-22, but that's . . . No. That's not right. I dip my head lower, feeling my brow furrow as my brain rakes and sifts through every plane, every engine, every roar I've ever chronicled. Shaking my head at last, I let out a frustrated snarl.

For the first time in ages, I cannot figure out what kind of plane this is.

I shield my eyes from the newly risen sun and look up to behold a yellow biplane with blue and red accents. As the plane soars overhead, I commit every stunning curve and throaty rumble to memory.

I will find out what kind of plane it is.

I fold myself into the driver's seat through the open window—the driver's-side front door has been busted for months now—buckle up, and turn the key in the ignition. The engine hums to life as I skim the directions I'd written out and compare them against my dog-eared map, tongue poking between my teeth in concentration as I trace out the remainder of my route. It'll take me another thirty minutes to get there, and I will still be about two hours early. I tuck my creased directions under the guide, turn on the radio, and begin the delicate dial dance of finding a good station to listen to for the rest of the drive. Whether I'll be able to get good reception on these mountain roads is anybody's guess.

Just as I think I've found a promising station that plays top-forty hits, a black blur followed by a huge wake of dust nearly sideswipes me. I grip the radio dial and watch as the black blur speeds off down the vacant stretch of highway, followed closely by a little blue Honda. A ping of curiosity radiates through me, then the unmistakable feeling that something is wrong. *Leave it alone, Danvers,* my inner voice warns. *You're so close. Don't mess this up like you mess up everything else.*

Can't hurt it check it out though, right?

The radio station crackles through just as I'm putting the car into drive, the opening chords of a hit song clear as a bell. I check to make sure there are no more little blurs closing in on me, and take off after the two cars, my chase now inconveniently sound-tracked by some soapy ballad about the pitfalls of love. So not the vibe I need right now, radio.

As I close in on the little blue Honda and pull up alongside it, I can see big scrapes of black paint along the now-crumpled driver's side of the car; it looks like they extend all the way to the front end. The girl behind the wheel flicks her gaze over at me. I try my best to gesticulate *Are you okay?* and *What happened?* She thrusts her arm forward, revealing a wrinkled and stained fast food uniform, and mouths, *He hit me.* She then runs her little fingers in the air between us, a gesture I'm pretty sure means the black blur hit her car and ran. Her face morphs from anger to worry as her car begins to slow and sputter from the damage. She bangs the steering wheel over and over while her car continues to slow.

Oh, hell no. If there's one cause I'm hopeless against, it's the little blue Hondas of this world that get sideswiped and ditched by big black blurs. It's on.

I honk the horn and roll down my window. She looks at me. I point to me and then toward the black blur. Her face dissolves into sobs as she figures out what I said.

"Can you keep up?" I yell over the smooth tunes of the ballad. She nods and swipes at her newly determined tear-lined face. I give her a big thumbs-up. She valiantly returns it. I gun my Mustang and roar down the road. I see a sign for a highway on-ramp in about three miles, and suddenly I know exactly where the driver is headed. And, thanks to the map resting on my front seat that I've studied for hours on end, I figure out how I might be able to cut him off at the pass.

I bank right and make a sharp turn onto a winding mountain road. The little blue Honda is way behind me. When I speed around the next curve, I can see the black blur hurtling toward the upcoming freeway on-ramp. I look from the blur to the gas station signs cropping up on the horizon and slam my foot down on the gas pedal.

That's right about the time I hear the sirens.

"Good," I say, looking back to see that my driving has attracted the attention of a state trooper. I skid around the last curve and begin the descent to the frontage road, sirens wailing behind me. I finally get to the base of the mountain just in time to see the black blur pull up to the final stoplight before the freeway on-ramp. Up close, I notice that the black blur is in reality a rather expensive black Jaguar, and that it has been scratched and damaged and has scrapes of blue paint all down the side. The man driving the Jag actually has the audacity to rest his arm languidly out his open window, as he takes a long drag off his cigarette. My eyes dart from the Jag to the empty intersection, to the freeway on-ramp, to the corner gas station, and take a quick peek back at the now-closing-in state trooper.

There is only one thing to do.

I floor it and hurtle down into the empty intersection, approaching the Jag head-on and squealing to a stop just centimeters from its front bumper. I turn off my car, silencing the ballad, climb out my open window, and hop down.

"You hit and ran," I say coolly, walking over to Mr. Jaguar. The state trooper screeches to a halt behind me, sirens finally muted. I see the Jaguar guy weighing the pros of giving me a piece of his mind versus getting away from the state trooper.

"Move your car!" he finally screams, flicking the butt of his cigarette onto the road.

"Stop right there!" the state trooper calls out. And then a confused "Both of you?" As the trooper emerges from the car, I take in the fact that she's a woman.

"He hit and ran," I say, pointing at the man as he subtly begins to reverse down the road. I see the state trooper scan the Jaguar's damage.

"Why don't you just stop right there," the state trooper says to the man, her voice calm and cutting. He's still inching his car back. Does this guy actually think he can still get away? The state trooper merely arches an eyebrow. The man in the Jaguar huffs and puffs and finally puts his car into park, just as the little blue Honda clackers down from the mountain and comes to a sputtering rest at the gas station. The girl gets out of her car and runs over, her face still tear-stained.

"He hit my car," she says to the state trooper. "He came through the drive-through just as I got off my shift. He was trying to put ketchup on his fries—wasn't paying attention at all—and just ran right into me." The state trooper listens to the girl with one eye firmly focused on the man in the Jaguar, who is, once again, inching toward the freeway on-ramp.

"You"—the state trooper points to the man—"out of the car." I start to walk back over to my Mustang. "You"—the state trooper points to me—"sit on that curb."

"But—"

"Sit."

The state trooper takes everyone's statements, gets all of our information, and even gives the girl a hand with calling her insurance company and making introductions at the gas station so she can get her car fixed. An hour later, the Jaguar has been impounded, the man has been ticketed and taken into custody, the little blue Honda is being pushed into the gas station's garage, and the girl has used the garage's pay phone to call her mother. As she walks over to her mom's car, the girl looks back at me (still sitting on the curb as I was told, thank you very much) and waves, a smile playing on her features. I wave back.

The state trooper finally ambles over to me. I push myself up into a standing position, brush the dirt off my pants, and stick out one hand, making my voice as formal as it will go.

"Officer. My name is Carol Danvers. I'm starting at USAFA today. I have to—"

She ignores my outstretched hand and interrupts. "You broke—and I'm just throwing this number out there because I didn't see the full extent of your little mountain racing tour—but I'm pretty sure you broke at least five Colorado laws," she says. I look down at her badge. WRIGHT. Her hair is natural and closely cropped. Her light russet skin is wrinkled at the edges of her eyes from smiling—not at me, or here, but, you know, with other people in other places.

I jerk my thumb toward the backseat of her car, where Jaguar man is awaiting justice, arms crossed and glowering. "He hit and ran. He's the bad guy," I reason.

"So that makes you . . ."

"Not the bad guy?"

"Uh-huh." The state trooper pulls out her ticket book.

I begin to panic. "Please. I . . . I couldn't let him get away. I didn't think, I just—"

"Exactly. You didn't think."

"There was no time. He was getting away—" I'm about to launch into the myriad of reasons why what

I did was justified, and then maybe some quick back-story about how, yes, this is apparently a thing I do and that this state trooper isn't the first authority figure to break it to me that I have issues with maybe launching myself into things before I've really thought them through, and, no, it hasn't always worked out, but I never regretted doing it, not one time. But instead I just think about how today is supposed to be the day all my dreams come true, not the day I'm reminded that even in my dreams I'm still the same me.

I swallow hard. What if she writes me a ticket, and this does me in? What if USAFA kicks me out of the program before I've even begun? I finally come up with this: "Please. I was going to get to fly."

"You remind me a lot of me when I was your age," the state trooper says. I puff up a bit. "That's not a compliment."

"Oh, um—"

"Usually the smartest in the room? The fastest?" I nod along. "Yeah, me too. Here's the thing about that. When you think you know everything, when everything comes easy—"

"It's not easy," I say, unable to continue to hold my tongue through this little lecture. She waits. "Fine. It's *easy adjacent*. How's that?"

"Always an excuse ready when things go sideways. Which they will, more often than not—"

Now it's my turn to interrupt. "I think I'd rather just have the ticket," I say. A wry smile breaks across the state trooper's face. An efficient nod, and then she whips out her ticket book and a pen and starts writing. My heart sinks, but I try not to let my face show my fear.

"I'm going to let you off with a warning," the state trooper says, ripping the ticket from the book.

"Oh," I exhale. I didn't even realize I'd been holding my breath. "Thank y—" She hands me the ticket.

"Read it."

"So, it's an actual *warning* warning. I thought *warning* just meant to caution, not that there were actual"—the state trooper arches an eyebrow—"words," I finish lamely, then I shut up and read.

Scrawled on the ticket are three actual words: *Let yourself learn.* I thought a warning would be more ominous.

"Let myself learn?"

"You're going to make split-second decisions up there, and the thing that will get you—and your fellow airmen—killed the fastest is thinking you know everything."

"What does that—?"

"The best split-second decisions are rooted in knowledge. You can act fast and be impulsive because you know what you're doing. And you'll know what you're doing if you have the patience to let yourself learn. Just think about it like this. Every new thing you learn—and I mean, really learn—buys you some knee-jerk, spontaneous, seemingly rash decision up there." I'm just about to speak, when she cuts me off. "I know it's not as fun as speeding around a mountain road, but . . ." She waits. "Will you do that for me?"

"Yes, ma'am."

She nods. "Then good luck up there, Danvers."

CHAPTER 2

I GO FROM BEING YELLED AT ON A BUS, TO BEING
yelled at standing next to the bus, to being yelled at
to walk away from the bus, and then we're yelled at to
stand in lines and drop our duffle bags and to definitely not look any of the cadet cadre in the eye when
they're talking to us. The din and the chaos, the yelling and hundreds of kids scrambling to follow orders
becomes white noise in no time at all. And then we're
being yelled at to walk—*no, not that way, walk this way*—into
a stately looking building where we're yelled at some
more. We're called *rainbows* and *doolies* and *basics* and *cadets*
and *trainees* and every other iteration in between. We
don't even get to be called airmen until the very end
of Basic after the Acceptance Parade. I mean, we don't

even get a name tape with our last name on it until week three.

I keep my eyes forward and survive in this part of myself that exists solely on pure excitement and the absolute terror of putting a foot wrong. I follow, I do as I'm told, and I keep reminding myself not to blurt out to the other cadets, *Can you believe we're finally here?! Isn't it great?!*

I've still not been able to compose a single thought, other than an internal high-pitched squeal of delight, when a group of us are funneled into a smaller room to take our Oath of Enlistment.

"Raise your right hand and repeat after me," the officer says. He's young, with white-blond hair that's cut short, and ice-blue eyes that bore into and seem to scan through every last one of us. He's way too cute not to know it. A quick glance at his badge. JENKS.

"I, state your full name," Officer Jenks says. We all repeat the first word and then the room is filled with a cacophony of all of our names being said at once. I say "CAROL DANVERS" as loudly and clearly as I can, feeling a flash of pride.

Jenks waits.

"Having been appointed a cadet in the United States Air Force—" As we follow and repeat what Jenks says through the remainder of the oath, I find that the words are getting caught in my throat. This is real. I am part of something bigger than myself. As we wind our way through to the final words, I realize I'm getting a bit choked up. *Keep it together, Danvers.*

"So help me God," Jenks says.

"So help me God," I repeat, allowing my eyes to drift shut as I get lost in the moment. This is it. Everything I've ever wanted is right within my—

"Danvers!" Officer Cadet Chen, her title referring to a military trainee studying to become a fully commissioned officer, appears as if from nowhere. The Officer Cadets here are often just called "OCs," for brevity.

"Yes, ma'am," I say, my eyes wrenching open and my voice clipped and efficient.

"Would you like to take the oath again?" I'm probably a good six inches taller than Officer Cadet Chen. And yet there's no doubt in my mind that she could defeat me—and definitely humiliate me—in every possible way. Her black hair is cut short, and her voice is disarmingly composed. Her face is serene as she waits for my reply.

"No, ma'am," I say, unsure of why I'm being asked.

"Well then, where is your flight, Basic?"

I look around the room and feel my face heat.

My flight is long gone. Since we got here, the thousand-strong class of basic cadets has been divided into smaller and smaller groups by the cadet cadre of upperclassmen. Each division has resulted in less and less anonymity. This is not a welcome realization. One thousand became ten one-hundred-cadet squadrons. And then those one hundred became thirty. And then those thirty became my flight. And in my flight, there are only four women. But right now, it's just me, Officer Cadet Chen, Officer Jenks, and the stolen moment that got me into this mess.

"Can you please do your job and get her out of here?" Jenks's voice is an indifferent sigh.

"Yes, sir," Chen says. She takes a breath before unleashing the hounds of hell. But just as she's about to speak, Jenks raises a single leisurely hand. Chen immediately stops, standing at attention as he walks over to me. I am still, staring forward. Jenks walks around me. I can hear his breathing and the squeak of his shoes. The hairs on the back of my neck stand on end as he comes to a stop in front of me. Jenks's lip curls in disappointment as he takes my measure.

"They'll let anyone in these days," Jenks comments. His gaze slides from me over to Chen. "Truly anyone."

Chen's eyes stay forward, but I notice the flicker as his words strike her right in the chest.

The next flight enters to take their Oath of Enlistment and Jenks dismisses both Chen and me with a wave of his hand. We turn on our heels and exit the room, Jenks having stripped Chen of any power she had. In that room—and in Jenks's eyes—we are both equally disappointing.

Chen appears to regain her composure as we enter the hall and rejoin the rest of the flight. No one looks up when I walk in with Chen hot on my heels. I know they're just relieved that they didn't get singled out. As I settle into line, I see Chen and Officer Cadet Resendiz share a look. Resendiz knows something happened and the look he gives her is one of both understanding and apology. He knows what kind of man Jenks is. Does everyone?

I scan the room and notice that the male cadets are in the process of getting their heads shaved, chunks of curls and strands of hair hitting the ground whisper-soft, like a first snowfall. I follow Chen to the area where the women can opt for a short cut—unless, like me, they have spent the last two years growing their hair out so that it'll all pull back into a tight bun that's a maximum of three inches in circumference and doesn't touch the top of the collar. Which meant I was obsessed with measuring, rulers, and optimizing rubber bands versus bobby pins over the past two years. I've even timed myself. These are the kinds of things that I thought about while my fellow high school peers nervously filed college applications and planned their big graduation parties.

After the hair line, Officer Cadets Chen and Resendiz direct us to move into the medical portion of today's events, where we're poked and prodded with impunity. I have no idea how much time has passed, but it feels like forever ago that I was sitting on the hood of my car, staring up at the Colorado sunrise, and listening for planes.

Chen and Resendiz then lead us to get our airman battle uniforms, and as the sky begins to grow dusky with nightfall, they finally take the group of us, drained and overcome, back to our luggage, and from there, to our dormitories. Chen stops in front of an open door.

"Danvers. Rambeau." I step forward, as does one of the other three women in my flight who I've seen hurtling through today's events. We don't dare look at each other. We stare straight ahead until Chen tells us what to do. Which, in the end, she does not. So we continue to stand. Chen stops in front of the room next door and barks out the other two women's names. All four of us are paralyzed. Do we walk in, do we—?

"First Beast begins tomorrow. I suggest you get some sleep." Chen strides down the hallway without another word.

The four of us look to one another, and then, before someone pops out and yells at us again, we all head quickly into our respective dorm rooms.

"Carol Danvers," I say, once we're safely inside, extending a hand to my new roommate.

"Maria Rambeau," she says, taking my outstretched hand. Her grip is strong and sure, and even though she's clearly exhausted like me, she looks me in the eye and I can feel her curiously searching my face for some way to measure what kind of person I am. I try to smile, try to tighten my grip, try to . . . well, impress her. Maria's deep umber skin glistens with sweat earned from a long day, and as her impossibly big brown eyes scan my face I feel as though she's on the cusp of slamming down some kind of psychological gavel as she finishes discerning my character and passes a verdict.

"Do you have a preference?" I blurt out, gesturing to the two beds.

"No." And then with an almost imperceptible head tilt, "Do you?"

"I'm sure they're both just as aggressively uncomfortable," I say. A tired smile breaks across Maria's face, and the joy that bursts through me could power downtown Colorado Springs.

"I'll take this one, then," Maria says, pointing to the bed on the right. I nod and we spend the next hour setting up our respective areas in silence. We measure and fold and buff, making sure to get as ready as possible for tomorrow, as well as prepare for any impending dorm inspections.

As I brush my teeth at the very end of the night, I can't remember eating or drinking anything today. But I know I must have. I know I saw a whole bunch of faces and said the words *yes, sir* and *no, ma'am* at least a thousand times. I know my blood was drawn and I took an oath to serve this country to the best of my ability, where I garnered the unfortunate attention of Jenks.

I spit out my toothpaste and rinse my mouth. In the calm and quiet of the bathroom, I rest my hands on the cold sink and close my eyes. I try to remember the sound of the mystery plane from this morning. Its high singsongy hum and the throaty groan of its engine. I make myself commit the sound to memory like it's a lullaby. A lullaby reminding me that I'm still me, through all this. Just a girl who would rather count planes than sheep to fall asleep at night.

I gather up my things and head back into the dorm room, where I find Maria sitting cross-legged on her bed writing in a journal. I smile as I close the door behind me, and she responds in kind. I want to say something to her, ask her what she wants to be when she grows up, if this is the endgame or just a stepping-stone, and whether she's nervous or scared or excited or maybe all three. But then it dawns on me that I don't think even I know the answers to those questions myself.

My favorite high school history teacher once told me that it was a mistake to make resolutions based on what I'm not. She said it's way easier for a group of people to come together in their shared hatred for something than it is to come together over their love of something or someone. But in the end, the group brought together by hatred will always be weaker.

Now I see that her point was that love is always stronger in the end. But the thing about love, especially loving yourself for who you are . . . It's harder than hating yourself for who you're not. Especially when you're eighteen. I know I didn't fit in back home. I know I was hated, or at least misunderstood, more for who I *wasn't* than loved for who I *was*. And what I want to tell Maria, what I want to tell myself, is that I hope I do more than just fit in here. I hope I *belong*. I hope I am loved.

For once.

I'm shuffling my toiletries around, doing some last-minute preparations for tomorrow, and then I can't hold it in any longer.

"A lot of yelling today," I say, my back turned to Maria. I don't want to see her become annoyed that I'm trying to talk to her. When the silence in the room goes on for half a second too long, I force myself to turn around. Maria is chewing on the end of her pen, looking over at me. Her face is . . . I don't know. . . . I don't know her well enough to read her face yet.

"Yeah," she finally says. *Ooookay.* I force a tight smile and nod.

"You ready for lights-out?" I ask, slowly dying inside. Maria nods that she is and sets her journal and pen on her desk and slides under the covers. She twists and turns, flips around as though she's trying to get comfortable. Finally . . .

"Hit it." I turn out the lights and Frankenstein my way over to the bed, shuffling and sliding my feet along the floor of the darkened dorm room, careful not to stub or hit anything in the process. It feels like the journey from the light switch to my bed takes me close to an hour. I finally crawl into bed, settle in on my left side—as usual—and try to fluff the thin standard-issue pillow under my head. The room falls into silence as I rue the day I decided to say something and not just play it cool. When will I ever learn—?

"Today was the best day of my life," Maria says, cutting through the deafening silence. Her voice quiet and clear. I smile so big you can see it from space.

"Mine too."

"Night, Danvers."

"Night, Rambeau."

P-51D Mustang, Piper Saratoga, Beechcraft, Cessna, Marchetti . . .

CHAPTER 3

ITS STILL DARK OUTSIDE WHEN I WAKE TO THE sound of Maria lacing up her sneakers.

"Did I miss Reveille?" I half shout, frantically pawing in the dark for my watch, already panicked. When I finally find it, the watch reads a truly upsetting 3:23 a.m.

"No, you've still got about an hour," she says, sliding on the other sneaker.

"You going running?" I ask. Even in the dark, I can see her look over at me with that same discerning head tilt. I understand that my question was at best an obvious one and at worst, downright stupid. "Right. What I meant was . . . I want . . . Can I come? Do you want company?"

"If you can get ready in the next seven minutes, you're welcome to join me, Danvers," she says, tying up her other sneaker. I bolt upright and make my bed using a ruler and hyper-focused concentration.

As I drag my sneakers out of my closet, the ticket I got from State Trooper Wright floats out of my duffle bag and onto the floor. Maria picks it up and hands it back to me, her face asking a question she doesn't give voice to. I take the ticket, shove it back into my duffle bag, sit on the bed, and start tying my sneakers.

"On my way here I had a little run-in with the law," I say, finishing lacing up one sneaker. Maria waits. "But she left me off with a warning. Or really more of a piece of advice. 'Let yourself learn.' Wrote it on the ticket so I guess I'd really . . . you know, be reminded of it."

" 'Let yourself learn'?" Maria asks.

"Yeah, it's—"

"Like . . . about yourself?"

"I—hmm. Welp, that's an angle I hadn't even thought of," I say, shaking my head.

"How else did you think of it?" Maria asks as we walk toward the PT pad, the night air quiet and tranquil around us.

"I figured she was talking about Air Force stuff." We settle onto the track and start our stretches. I notice two cadets from another flight on the other side of the track stretching just like we are.

"Air Force stuff?" Maria asks, unable to keep from smiling.

"That's the official name for it, right?" I laugh.

"Oh, definitely. I think I saw it on a poster in the recruitment center." Maria extends her hand high into the sky and then arches her arm as she speaks. " 'Aim high and learn Air Force stuff'!" I crumble into giggles as I touch my toes, feeling a nice stretch down my back.

"You run track in high school?" I ask, my voice cutting off slightly as I fold into myself.

"A little," Maria says, but from her half grin I discern that "a little" is probably the understatement of the century. "You?"

"A little," I say, following her lead. She smiles full-on this time, jumping in the air a few times, her breath puffing in the space between us.

Our pace is comfortable. Neither one of us wants to burn out before this morning's first physical evaluation. We're going to be timed on our one-and-a-half-mile run, one minute of push-ups, one minute of sit-ups, and one minute of pull-ups.

As we round the first corner, the syncopation of our steps feels almost meditative. I wouldn't mind starting every morning like this. The quiet normalcy of another day running in the brisk morning air, just like I used to back home. I hadn't even thought of a daily run as a possible part of the new routine, the new *me*.

I thought I had to leave everything behind that made me . . . me. I thought I'd be stronger without the baggage of my past. Like a condemned house that was bulldozed for the land, ready to make way for a fancier new house. A better house. Why didn't it ever occur to me that what got me here could be the same thing that would make me do well?

Breathing deep from my diaphragm, I think about the state trooper's words and Maria's interpretation: *Let yourself learn.* Why didn't I get that those words could also apply to learning about myself? Not to remake myself or to build a *new* me, but to unearth more of the real me within. I thought that to become the Air Force's first female fighter pilot, I had to become someone else. But I'm capable of so much more. I'm starting to think that it's *this* me that'll make history.

I feel stronger than ever as we come around for another lap. Maria and I begin to keep pace with the two cadets from another flight, one man and one woman. I bet they thought they'd be able to lap us. But it seems they're the ones on the brink of getting lapped. Maria and I exchange a knowing look as we float past them in the final leg of our last lap. We make sure to appear as unexhausted as possible as we slow to a jog for our final cooldown.

Slowly but surely, the rest of the class starts streaming out to the PT pad. Maria and I fall in with the rest of our flight. There are warm-ups, more yelling, and then we're readied for our first physical evaluation.

I'm starting to get some last names for the fellow cadets in my flight. Bianchi is, or believes that he is, the clear leader. Lanky and effortlessly athletic, the confidence oozes off him. His dewy no-blemish-in-sight olive-hued skin sets off what was once a thick mop of wavy black hair, and he wields his deep blue eyes like tractor beams. Even after only one day, Bianchi already has two other airmen, Del Orbe and Pierre, following him around. I notice him trying to calculate where Maria and I fall into his little pecking order. He still seems unsure. I hope to offer him some clarity on this point in the very near future.

The two cadets from the other flight that were there on the track with us this morning are Johnson and Noble. Noble is one of only two women in her flight. I catch myself storing all these names and possible alliances and habits and traits in the back of my mind, like they're part of some elaborate blackboard algorithm. Something about collecting data on these people makes me feel, however falsely, more in control.

I find myself sticking close to Maria. And I don't think I'm wrong in believing that she's doing the same thing with me.

Flight after flight are called up and evaluated. Our flight is up next.

OCs Chen and Resendiz round us up and give us the rundown of what's about to happen. As the evaluations begin, so does the competition among cadets. Timed push-ups. Timed sit-ups. Timed pull-ups. By the time we get to the mile-and-a-half run, it's Maria, Bianchi, Pierre, and me in the lead. Pierre and Bianchi had the upper hand in pull-ups, but Maria had more push-ups than both of them and I had more sit-ups. As we line up at the start of the run, none of us look at each other, all four of us staring straight ahead, visualizing the end goal.

GO!

We all burst off the line. I cut to the inside as fast as I can and draft off Pierre. My breathing is easy and my legs have never felt stronger. The chaos and madness fall away, and I find myself smiling and almost laughing as I burst out to the front of the pack. The measuring of the sheets and the folding of the towels within a millimeter and the reporting statements and all the rest fade into the background as I pull away. Of all the things I can't control, everything that's unknown, me running fastest around this track is not one of them. I don't know who's behind me or how close they are, but within three laps I can't hear anything but my own rhythmic pace and my own steady exhalations. By the time I surge over the finish line, I can't keep from smiling. I slow to a jog and then a full stop, bend over, and rest my hands on my knees as I catch my breath. It's another two seconds before Maria comes across the finish line. Bianchi and Pierre finish a distant third and fourth. Both were an entire half lap behind the two of us. Maria walks over to me, hands on her hips.

"So you ran track a little, huh?" Maria says, laughing.

"Yeah, well, right back at'cha," I say, straightening my posture.

"I don't know what I loved more, watching the other

flights see us finish first and second, or catching the exact moment Bianchi realized he lost," Maria says haltingly as she catches her breath.

"You clocked him, too?" I ask, my voice dipping into a low whisper.

"Dudes like Bianchi are a dime a dozen," Maria says. She mimes a giant yawn. "Boring."

"He can be as boring as he wants, as long as he doesn't get in the way of me being able to fly combat," I say, my voice an unguarded lilt. And then it all happens so fast. I can see Maria's face light up at my words and then immediately fall as her focus is pulled to something—or to be exact, someone—just behind me. It takes milliseconds for me to turn around and see that they've heard me. Bianchi, Pierre, and Del Orbe, who's also finished his run, have heard me say something that I've never said out loud until this very moment.

"Women don't fly combat, Danvers," Bianchi says.

"Yet," I counter.

"Is now really the time you want to be telling women what they can and can't do?" Maria asks, stepping between Bianchi and me. " 'Cause I could have sworn this morning you were talking a lot of mess about how women would be trailing . . . what was it?"

"A full lap behind him," Pierre finishes. Bianchi shoots him a look.

"A full lap behind you," Maria repeats.

"And who was it that was a full lap behind?" I ask, scratching my head dramatically for emphasis. Bianchi walks up to me. Close. I lift my chin in defiance and don't flinch.

"You come in first all you want, Danvers. I still get to be a fighter pilot and you don't." Bianchi's voice is a melodic whisper. He leans in closer. "Congratulations."

"Danvers! Bianchi! Fall in!" Our entire group leaps to action, as OCs Chen and Resendiz gather our flight to go back to the dorms so we can take showers before breakfast and begin a day filled with briefings, classes, and being yelled at about things I thought I knew how to do, like putting my arms in the right place while walking.

My body is tight and hard as I await instruction. My jaw is bolted shut and my pulse is deafening as it pounds inside my head.

You come in first all you want, Danvers. I still get to be a fighter pilot and you don't.

We march to breakfast in synchronized perfection. My own precision is being fueled by a barely tamped-down rage that's verging on apocalyptic. As we reach Mitchell Hall, my eye line has pinholed to just the nape and shoulders of the person in front of me. By the time Maria and I are able to start eating, I'm seething.

"Did you really mean what you said?" Maria asks, her voice low as we move through the line, piling our trays with fruit and complex carbs to refuel for the day ahead.

"About what?"

"That you wanted to fly combat?"

"Yes." My voice chokes out and I can hear both the desperation and frustration at the same time. "It's all I've ever wanted." I ball up my fists and feel the tension in my shoulders building and building and building. Maria's eyes widen as though she can sense the impending storm, and she hands me a bread roll from her tray.

"Scream into it. Usually I use a pillow, but . . . desperate times. It's what I do after encounters with guys like Bianchi." I take Maria's bread roll, lift it to my face, and take a giant bite out of it. She laughs.

"Thank you," I say, my mouth full.

"Feel better?"

"No."

"Because he's right?"

"Yeah."

Maria and I stare off into the middle distance.

"Maybe not, though," I say. Maria looks over. "Pilots are ranked on flying skills, leadership, and adaptability. The top pilots get the best assignments. We get to pick between bombers, tankers, transport, trash haulers, helicopters—"

"And fighter jets."

I nod. "If we're the top two in our class and we get into the airmanship program . . . I don't know . . . maybe we have a shot."

"The Flying Falcons," Maria pronounces, slurping up a spoonful of oatmeal.

"What are the Flying Falc—"

Our conversation grinds to a halt as one of the cadet cadre materializes over Maria, yelling about table manners and too much chewing. We all understand why they're so harsh in these beginning weeks of Basic. It's not about whatever tiny infraction has gotten you singled out, it's about discipline and performing under pressure and keeping a level head while you follow orders. If you can keep your cool when someone's telling you your salute needs to pop from here, not there, and to do it again and again and again, then you'll probably be better equipped to accomplish what needs to be done when lives are at stake. There's always a bigger picture.

It's only at the end of the day, when we finally return to our dorm room, that Maria and I can pick our conversation back up. The door closes behind us and Maria hurries over and starts sifting through all the orientation paperwork neatly organized on her desk. She pulls a pamphlet out with a victorious flourish.

"The Flying Falcons." Maria shoves the paper toward me and triumphantly slams her hands onto her hips as I read.

" 'The Flying Falcons are an elite nine-member flying squadron based out of the United States Air Force Academy. Founded in 1963, the Flying Falcons compete with other intercollegiate squadrons to further the Air Force's legacy of greatness and demonstrate that the sky is no limit. Aim high!' "

"Anyone can apply," Maria says, taking back the pamphlet.

"Even women?"

"Yeah." Maria flips through the pages. "I mean, at least . . . it doesn't say we can't."

"And you think—"

"If we're the top two in our class and we get into the airmanship program AND we make it onto the

Flying Falcons?" Maria finishes my train of thought as she counts off each of the items on what is fast becoming our shared to-do list for the year. Her three raised fingers hang in the air between us.

"How can they say no?" I wonder.

"They can't."

"They'll try," I say.

Maria's eyes sparkle. "Let them."

CHAPTER 4

COUNTLESS HOURS OF LATRINE DETAIL.

An untold number of push-ups.

Limitless write-ups and yelled orders.

Morning after morning of making my bed with the same ruler.

Days spent cursing that one speck of dust way up on the top shelf that got me a stern reprimand on my first dorm inspection.

Memorizing every detail of Chen's and Resendiz's faces so we can figure out whether that eye twitch is a good or a bad thing.*

Maria and I continue to run in the dark early

---

*It's a bad thing.

morning hours. And even though Pierre has joined us now and then, Bianchi's campaign against Maria and me rages on.

His crusade comes to a head during week three in our Introduction to Air Force Combatives class when Bianchi and I are paired off. The match ends when he stomps off after being forced to concede I won. As we sit along the wall once he returns to the gym, I try to reason with him. I figure if we could just talk—one on one—he'll see how much energy he's wasting on making enemies out of Maria and me. I think he'll come around for sure.

"We're all on the same side here," I say, offering Bianchi a towel.

"I don't need a pep talk from you," he seethes.

"Then what do you need?" I really want to know. He shakes his head. "You think this will get better if I let you win?"

"No one lets me win."

"No kidding."

"I win on my own." I arch an eyebrow. He grits his teeth. "Not here specifically, but I have, in the past. . . . You know what I mean."

"Why does it matter so much to you?"

"Why does it matter so much to *you*?" Bianchi shoots back.

"Because unlike you, some of us have a lot to prove." We both watch as Maria pins Pierre, her legs wrapping around his neck as the match is called. "I'm not saying you're handed things, I see how hard you work. But now imagine what it'd be like to work that hard and do that well and still not be considered for combat."

Bianchi sits back against the wall, heaving a sigh. "It's not personal, Danvers."

"Sure feels personal."

As Bianchi gets quiet, I think of a million better comebacks. Intelligent, layered, illuminating arguments that'll make him get what it's like to be excluded from doing something that others take for granted. In the end, Bianchi and I just sit there in silence until it's time to leave. And then we never speak about it again.

But even with the run-ins with Bianchi, and the latrine detail and the push-ups and the cursed speck of dust and the reprimands and the laps around the track and the cold judgments from the other men in our flight who, while not quite Bianchi-level, aren't exactly welcoming, Maria and I end every day talking about a life spent in the clouds as fighter pilots in the United States Air Force. It keeps us going, keeps us strong and focused.

Most important, it keeps us dreaming.

At breakfast, Maria sets down her tray across from me. The rest of the flight is deep in conversation as she takes her first sip of coffee. I swirl my now-lukewarm tea around in my mug and wait to bombard her with everything I've learned. Maria peels the wrapper off a muffin, takes a bite, and closes her eyes in ecstasy. I stifle a laugh. It's incredible how delicious normally average mess hall food becomes when your body is constantly craving calories thanks to endless physical exertion.

It's the final day of First Beast. Tomorrow we leave for Jacks Valley. The three weeks we'll endure out there in the wild will make these first four weeks of Basic look like kindergarten.

I can't wait.

But today? Today is Field Day.

Today is the day when our flight joins forces with the upperclassmen and finally forms our full squadron. After that, all the squadrons compete against one another in events ranging from classic tugs-of-war, steeplechases, and relay races, all the way to log carries and long-distance runs. With the bleachers full of the cadets' families and the top USAFA brass, it's a day to

blow off some steam, have some fun, and show everyone what we're made of.

"I'm going to miss these muffins when we go," Maria
laments. I am able to wait three more whole seconds.
And, yes, I do deserve a medal.

"Jenks is in charge of the Flying Falcons," I say,
blurting out the information that took me weeks to
gather.

"The 'they'll let anyone in these days' guy?"

"Yep."

She snorts. "Well, that's inconvenient."

"Yes, but what if we come in first at Field Day? We'd
get Honor Squadron and—"

"Us winning Honor Squadron isn't going to change
this guy's mind," Maria cuts me off. She sets down her
muffin and brushes the crumbs off her fingertips.

"It might sway him? Just mooooove him over a little
bit?" But Maria is already shaking her head.

"If we set out to win Honor Squadron, then we need
to be doing it for ourselves," Maria says.

"And maybe . . . like twenty percent to rub Jenks's
nose in it," I wheedle.

"Twenty percent?"

"Just twenty percent for nose rubbing," I confirm.
Maria nods her head as she takes a swig of orange juice.

"So, Jenks walks over to congratulate us on our big win through gritted teeth and we say, 'Hello, hi, yes, Captain Jenks. We, members of this *Honor Squadron* and numbers one and two in this cadet class, respectively—'"

"'Respectively,'" I echo.

"'—would like very much like to apply for your Flying Falcons elite nine-member squad, and in so doing mayhap become the first women to fly combat.'"

"'Mayhap'?"

"I'm being swept away, can you just . . . let me live?"

There is a beat.

"Mayhap," I confirm.

"But to win Honor Squadron we've got to rally the troops." My eyes flick over toward Bianchi, Pierre, and Del Orbe. Maria polishes off the last bite of her beloved muffin.

"They'll come around. Winning is winning."

Our squadron is the Aggressors. We've donned light blue shirts for today's festivities, assigned to our group by the powers that be. All around us the other squadrons get ready for the opening ceremonies: The Barbarians in orange, the Cobras in purple, the Demons in green, the Executioners in navy, the Flying Tigers in red, the Guts in maroon, and then Hellcats in yellow.

OCs Chen and Resendiz walk us through how today will go and remind us which events we'll be taking part in. I've been put on the steeplechase, a race that involves lots of hurdles and water jumps, and Maria is on the long-distance run. She's also taking part in the tug-of-war. Pierre and Del Orbe are part of the team doing the log carry, and Bianchi and I are part of the relay race. We're a big squadron, and it's a testament to our abilities that Maria and I got assigned such plum events.

As we line up for opening ceremonies, Maria and I pull Bianchi, Pierre, and Del Orbe aside.

"What's up?" Bianchi asks.

"We want to win today," I say.

"So do we," Del Orbe says.

"Yes, but we have a bit of a teamwork problem," I say.

"Do you see where we're going with this?" Maria asks.

"You want us to play nice," Pierre says.

"We win, we all win. We lose . . ."

"You don't have to dramatically trail off," Bianchi says as I dramatically trail off. "We get it."

"Truce?" Maria asks. Bianchi, Pierre, and Del Orbe look to one another.

"Yeah, all right," Bianchi says, as Pierre and Del Orbe nod in agreement.

"Good," I say, but my eyes stay locked on Bianchi.

There's a moment of pause. Then: "You want me to say it, don't you?" Bianchi asks.

"A little," I admit.

"Just say it, man," Pierre says to Bianchi.

Bianchi extends his hand to Maria. "Truce," he says. They shake hands.

"Truce," Maria says.

"Now me," I say, extending my hand. Bianchi can only shake his head. He takes my hand in his.

"Truce," he says.

"Truce," I say.

"Truce," Del Orbe says to Maria.

"Truce," Maria says.

"Truce," I say to Pierre.

"Enough. That's . . . This is ridiculous," Bianchi says, even as a small smile plays around his mouth.

"FALL IN!" Chen yells, and we scatter.

Our squadron begins to stand out almost right away. Wherever I look, a light blue shirt is surging past and over and beyond all the other competitors. It's not just our speed—there's a synergy to our team. The unspoken ebbs and flows, the catches and releases, and understanding how we fit together as opposed to how we can win separately. We are at last egoless as we drive our team higher, farther, and faster than the others.

Now that I've come to know Bianchi, Pierre, and Del Orbe a little better, I understand why they're friends. This is a tough place to be on your own, and it makes sense that they bonded over competing with—and taking jabs at—Maria and me. But just as my history teacher said, their bond over a shared hatred was a weak one. Pierre had already been distancing himself from their group by week four. But now it feels like there's a lightness to us. Instead of allowing our differences to divide us and prompt distrust, we're stronger for putting aside our squabbles and uniting in a shared love of the game, and a desire to win.

On the opposite end of the spectrum, I see Johnson barking out orders to the rest of his Demon squadron, micromanaging, then deciding that he may as well do it himself, thereby cutting the spirit of the day off at the knees. That squadron progressively falls behind, weighted down with the heaviness of his animosity.

As we come to the final events, our squadron is in

the lead. By a lot. Apparently, this turn of events has unhinged Johnson even more. If that's even possible.

As Bianchi and I are walking over to the track for the relay, Johnson can no longer stand to stay quiet about all the many injustices in his life that have led him to today.

"Shouldn't you be playing softball?" He sneers at me as he catches up to us. "Figure skating, maybe?"

"Why? Do you want to get beat at those, too?" I hear Bianchi snort a laugh just behind me. We pick up our pace and continue on toward the starting line.

"Is that what I sounded like?" Bianchi asks, as we near the start.

"As if it's so far in your past," I joke. Bianchi goes quiet. "Oh, you're really asking?"

"I'm really asking."

"I used to waitress part-time in this little diner back home—"

"I can't figure out if you'd be an awful waitress or a great one," Bianchi interjects.

I nail him with a look. "Don't change the subject." Bianchi throws up his hands in surrender. "Like I was saying, I used to waitress. And whenever there was a baby crying in the diner, do you want to know what would stop them crying the fastest?"

"Something to eat? Picking them up?"

"Nope. It was when another baby started crying way louder."

Bianchi grimaces. "So, I'm the first crying baby in this scenario."

I grin back at him. "Well, yeah, but you're missing the point! The reason they stop crying is because when they're able to experience themselves, really see themselves? They stop."

Bianchi looks skeptical. "Is that science, Danvers, or conjecture?"

I shrug. "Hey, I'm no scientist, but in the diner my theory never led me wrong."

Bianchi's brow is furrowed in thought as we thread our way through the crowd that's bunched up around the starting line. "And I was a great waitress," I toss over my shoulder.

"Of course you were," Bianchi says, rolling his eyes. But it works; his mood lightens as we fall in with the upperclassmen from our squadron. I am the only woman in our squadron participating. They're setting the order based on our PT-evaluation times.

"I'm trying to decide whether to put you first or last," the upperclassman in charge says to me.

"Last," I say confidently. The upperclassman nods

and proceeds with assigning the rest of the positions. I scan the bleachers and find Jenks almost immediately. He's here and watching. Good.

The race begins. The upperclassman in charge of our squadron bursts off the line. He rounds the corner, and the race is tight. As he comes in to pass the baton, our team is a close third. The handoff is smooth, and our second leg is striding down the track with ease. Bianchi steps up to get ready for the third leg. I can feel Johnson watching as he figures out that it'll be me—not Bianchi—facing him in the final heat. The second leg comes in and hands off to Bianchi. I step onto the start line.

"Good luck," Johnson says, unable to help himself, his tone full of snark. I am quiet, concentrating. "Danvers. I said good luck," he repeats himself a little louder, but I ignore him. I watch as Bianchi moves us into second place, right behind Johnson's team.

Johnson and his mocking fall away as Bianchi rounds the corner. We lock eyes and suddenly the baton is hot in my hand. Then it's just me and the track. I pass Johnson easily. I allow myself a small smirk as I leave him in the dust. While I do love a withering comeback, most of the time actions really do speak louder than words.

This is not one of those breathtakingly tense races where I explode ahead right at the last moment. Not even close. After I glide past Johnson, I finish first by a long shot.

The Aggressors are named Honor Squadron. And for a few brief moments there's no yelling, no drilling, no marching, and no measuring sheets with a ruler. We're allowed to talk and laugh and congratulate one another. Bianchi and I share a genuine smile. The day is a beautiful clear one and the sun feels so good on my face.

I scan the group of USAFA dignitaries as they make their way through the crowd, congratulating each member of the Aggressors. Jenks is the last to come through, hanging back and taking his time. I look over at Maria. She sees him, too. The conversation between the VIPs and the Aggressors squadron is casual, for once. We're at ease, and for these brief moments of celebration, there is no *yes, sir* or *no, sir*. It's truly a once-in-a-lifetime opportunity.

Jenks extends his hand to me, the recollection of our brief encounter nowhere on his face at first, and then . . . I see him remember. His face drains of any civility as he steps toward Maria without a word.

"Well done out there, Rambeau," he says.

"Thank you, sir."

"I was particularly impressed with your leadership in the tug-of-war. I saw you reposition your team members just at the start. I couldn't quite hear what orders you were yelling, but they must have been spot-on," Jenks says.

"Our team fought hard, sir," Maria says. Jenks smiles and is about to walk away. "Sir, about the Flying Falcons." She motions to me. "We heard you're the one in charge."

"Yes?"

Maria squares her shoulders. "Well, we are interested in applying."

"The Flying Falcons tryout is open to anyone"—Jenks waits just long enough for Maria and I to share a look of excitement, before he adds—"with a private pilot's license."

"A private pilot's license?" Maria asks.

"Am I to assume, then, that you don't have one?" He asks, the condescension in his tone barely detectible.

Barely.

"No, sir," Maria says. Jenks slithers his gaze over to me.

"No, sir," I say.

"Such a shame." Jenks smiles.

"Yes, sir," Maria says. Her voice is flat.

"But chin up." Maria and I straighten. "The Flying Falcons are always looking for support." Jenks pauses. We wait. "From the ground."

"Yes, sir," Maria says firmly.

Jenks gives us one last thin-lipped smile and walks off the field with the rest of the higher-ups.

" 'From the ground,' " I slowly repeat Jenks's words.

"The pamphlet didn't say anything about a private pilot's license," Maria fumes.

"What are we going to do?" I ask.

"I don't know."

Maria and I are quiet, the day's victory paling in comparison to the stark disappointment of this moment.

Both of us are lost in thought, searching the horizon for an answer, a lightning bolt of an idea, or maybe even a private pilot's license. Every now and then we both shake our heads in frustration. We grind our teeth, put our hands on our hips and then drop them, pace and huff. Maria comes to a stop just in front of me.

"We'll find a way," I say, trying to boost us both. She nods and nods. And then a wide, ornery smile breaks across her face.

"We always do," she says.

CHAPTER 5

"WHAT ARE YOU TRYING TO PROVE?"

"You won't last a week!"

"You don't belong here!"

We're in the thick of Second Beast in Jacks Valley. I'm crawling under barbed wire, on my back, weapon in hand, and I can no longer remember a time in my life when I wasn't covered from head to toe in mud.

We run the assault course and compete against other cadets with pugil sticks. We learn basic first aid, which I put to use almost immediately as I leap, fall, and launch myself through the obstacle course. We are trained on our M16s and become very good at holding our weapons over our heads for long periods of time.

I try to hurl myself across a lake using a rope swing,

but I miss. I do it again and miss by less. I do it again, my fingers curling around the rope just long enough to give me a mean rope burn, and land, for the third time, in the icy water.

I successfully scale a six-foot wall—after seven tries.

Our flight is well on its way to earning Beast excellence (to add to our Honor Squadron). And the plan that Maria and I still have is to win all the awards, 80 percent for us, 20 percent for rubbing Jenks's nose in it.

To be honest, after our encounter with him on Field Day, it's more like 70 percent versus 30 percent.

This plan hinges on us getting the Warhawk, an award given only to the trainees who achieve the highest physical level, and then each of us cementing an Honor Graduate nod.

I sleep on a tiny cot in a giant tent out in the open. We eat our meals in a Quonset hut and fall asleep to the sounds of nature and snoring cadets.

It's. So. Great. I. Can't. Believe. It.

Maria and I sit at breakfast in the early-morning hours. The air around us is crisp and beautiful. We are quiet, staring off into space. As she takes a sip of her coffee with a sigh, I can only smile. There's a certain wonderfulness to that moment when you can just sit in silence with someone who's becoming a better and better friend. Maybe even a best friend.

I don't know what these weeks would have been like without Maria. No, I know exactly what these weeks would have been like without Maria.

Lonely. Painfully lonely.

I've never had a friend like Maria. I mean, I've had friends, but not ones I could totally be myself with. Back in school, there was the real me and then there was the version of me that I'd trot out for public consumption. I knew I wasn't being myself, but now that I've met Maria I can't believe I got by while giving so little.

"I can't feel my arms," Maria complains.

"I just feel soreness, and I'm assuming the soreness is where my arms are," I say, taking a long gulp of my tea.

Over the course of Second Beast, Maria and I have thrown out hundreds of possible scenarios to push through, drive past, or flat-out get around Jenks's whole private pilot's license setback. After doing some research, we found out that you need forty hours of flight time and to be able to pass an FAA-knowledge written test in order to get a pilot's license. The written test will be a piece of cake, but forty hours in the air? How are we supposed to get that before the Flying Falcon tryouts?

Maria and I have started to come to terms with the fact that we probably won't be able to apply to the Flying Falcons this year. If we get our private pilot's licenses over the summer, then we can try out for the Flying Falcons next year. It's not the best outcome, but at least now we have a plan.

Suddenly, OCs Chen and Resendiz are looming over us. It's time. Our lovely shared friend-silence will have to be put aside, because today is the day we cadets have all been dreading since long before we ever stepped foot on campus.

CBRN.

CBRN sounds like exactly what it is. These letters stand for Chemical, Biological, Radiological, and Nuclear. CBRN is an exercise where we must stand in an actual gas chamber, take off our gas masks, say our reporting statement, and then "calmly" exit the building, hoping we won't be the ones who throw up or pass out.

We're quiet as we arrive at the site, learn about our chemical-warfare gear, and are walked through every possible scenario that awaits us once we're inside. Trying to keep my head and not give in to my now-rampaging fear, I follow the group as we head down to the main building. Once there, we watch as flight after flight take up their positions in line.

"I hear it gets stronger and stronger with every group," Maria whispers.

I look around at the remaining flights. Johnson and Noble's flight is already in line, while we wait for Del Orbe to finish gearing up. Del Orbe's zipper has gotten caught and Bianchi—his wingman—won't leave him until all is well. And without Del Orbe and Bianchi, we can't get in line as a full flight. Del Orbe finally wrestles his zipper free, and Bianchi gives us all the high sign and we line up.

We are the last flight to go in.

As we stand in line, we can see a stream of cadets who've already gone through the gas chamber exiting the back of the building. Their arms are outstretched, their reddened faces are dripping with snot and tears. Every once in a while, a cadet lurches over and vomits as efficiently as possible, trying not to call too much attention to themselves. I notice that I've gone into a mode that even I have only seen a few times before. Hyper-focused, every brain cell fixated on surviving the next ten minutes.

I remember one of the mantras I used to recite on

the track team whenever my legs would burn as I tried to push faster than I ever had before, or run a new personal best: *I can do anything for ten minutes!* I'd repeat it over and over in my head with every step, reminding myself that whatever pain I was feeling was temporary.

"We can do anything for ten minutes," I whisper to Maria, who's lined up in front of me. She doesn't turn around, but I can see her nod. They open up the doors and we are finally ushered inside.

Our flight lines one wall until the commanding officer in the center of the room tells us to start doing jumping jacks, or anything else to raise our heart rates. Maria and I both run in place, throwing in a jumping jack here or there. Almost immediately I can feel the burning just around my hairline, right where the sweat has started forming. The stinging moves to the nape of my neck and all around the area where my gas mask is. My breathing is getting more and more erratic as the gas fills the room. I try to stay calm. Focus on my breathing. Focus on one foot hitting the floor and then the other. I try to convince myself that the burning is just an itch as it prickles down my back, but it's getting worse. The commanding officer orders us to loosen the elastic bands on our gas masks and get ready to take off the whole thing. He instructs us to hold the gas masks at our chests once we take them off, recite our reporting statement, and then calmly walk out of the building with our arms outstretched like a T. If we run, he says, we will have to do it all over again. This is when the mantra *Don't run* eclipses *I can do anything for ten minutes*. There's no way I'm doing this again.

The commanding officer tells us to take off our gas masks.

The gas hits me like a tidal wave of acid. It's everywhere. I blink and blink, trying not to gulp down any more gas than what's currently burning its way down my throat. I clutch the gas mask to my chest and recite my reporting statement in an eerily calm voice. Tears and snot run down my face as I turn toward the exit and follow Maria out of the building, both of us extending our arms into a T position as instructed. Once outside, I walk the two laps around the building that we're supposed to. I see Pierre fold over and throw up so violently that he's almost curled into a kneeling position.

"You okay?" Maria rasps at me as we round the corner on our second lap.

"Yeah," I gasp. "You?"

"That was worse than I thought it would be," she says, blinking and blinking through her tears. We pass Pierre again, and he's still doubled over. Maria and I look at each other and at the same moment, make a beeline over to him.

"Come on," I say, taking his right side while Maria pulls up his left. He grunts out a thanks as we lead him over to where everyone is rinsing out their masks. His gas mask has left a bright red mark on his tawny skin, right at the base of his hairline, and his brown eyes are bloodshot and welling with tears. Clutched in his hand are his chunky black glasses, now caked in vomit. He swipes at his nose, hoping to take some of the snot with it. But there's plenty more where that came from.

"At least it's taken care of my cold," Pierre finally manages to say, as we sit with our Meal, Ready-to-Eats, also known as MREs, later that afternoon. He breathes in deeply. "Completely cleared up."

"At least it's over," Maria says, taking a long drink of water. "I'd been dreading that since . . . I mean, since before I even applied to the Academy."

"Me too, Rambeau. I'd heard horror stories," Pierre says.

"I'm Maria. That's Carol," Maria says to Pierre, jerking her thumb in my direction. "By the way."

"Garrett," he says, laughing. "I didn't even . . . It

never occurred to me that I didn't know anyone's first names."

"It's not like we're ever going to call each other by them," I say.

"Right?" Maria agrees. I look over just as Bianchi and Del Orbe make their way to us.

"Can we join you?" Bianchi asks, gesturing to the ground right next to us. All of us nod or sweep our arms in a welcoming manner. Fine. It's me who does the sweeping. I don't know what else to do.

"We were just saying we didn't know each other's first names," I say. Bianchi takes a big bite of his food. "Not that we'd ever use them, but . . ."

"Might be nice to know them," Maria prompts. Bianchi and Del Orbe nod, but don't volunteer right away.

"Carol," I say, deciding to set the tone.

"Maria."

"They already know mine." Pierre takes a drink of water from his canteen. "I figured I should probably tell them because they helped me over my vomitfest just after my wingman straight up left me."

"My name's Erik," Del Orbe says, smiling. He has the deepest dimples I've ever seen. And then all eyes are on Bianchi.

"Tom," Bianchi says, begrudgingly.

"That is unexpected," Maria says, snickering.

"What? Why?" Bianchi says.

"You just . . . don't look like a Tom," I say.

"You look like a Brad," Pierre blurts out. Everyone nods and laughs.

"Brock," Maria says.

"Chip," I say.

"Laaaaaance," Del Orbe says, unable to keep from laughing. Del Orbe has one of those great cackling, leaning-all-the-way-back, mouth-fully-open sort of laughs.

Bianchi only nods, turning red around the ears, as we continue to tease him with names.

Finally we grow tired of our game, and as Del Orbe, Pierre, and Maria fall into conversation about the upcoming Acceptance Parade, I turn to Bianchi.

"You didn't leave Del Orbe," I say. Bianchi looks over. "Earlier. When his zipper got stuck."

"I'm his wingman," he says, simply.

CHAPTER 6

MARIA AND I MAKE OUR WAY DOWN TO THE parade field dressed in our blues. We've taken all our tests and had our evaluations. We've been drilled on the inverted-wedge formation that we'll march in during today's festivities about as many times as we've been told that we'll only be marching in the inverted-wedge formation two times in our entire Air Force career: once on Acceptance Day, and once when we graduate from USAFA.

Today is the first time. After thirty-seven days of Basic Training, I'll march in the Acceptance Parade and, as a fourth-class cadet, will finally be called Airman Danvers.

I've never been more proud of anything in my entire life.

As we fall in with the rest of our flight, I'm nervous and excited. I walk into today's Acceptance Parade knowing I have done what I need to do to be on track to become the Air Force's first female fighter pilot. Or at least, one of them.

Maria and I were both awarded the Warhawk. Our flight was presented with the Honor Flight, and earned the Beast flight back in Jacks Valley. And out of all those honors, Maria and I were singled out as two of just eight of the cadets to be named an Honor Graduate.

Our plans to try out for the Flying Falcons this year may never reach fruition. And Jenks might very well be secretly reveling in that possibility. But at least I've kept up my end of the bargain by successfully spending at least a portion of today's festivities relishing in Jenks getting his nose 30 percent rubbed in Maria's and my (now well-documented) excellence. I know Maria is right and that nothing we do will change his mind, but it doesn't mean that I'm going to stop trying.

The gathered crowd of USAFA luminaries and cadets' families number in the thousands. Noisy and celebratory, every step we take is met with tear-filled sobs from proud parents juggling signs and flowers for their cadets. I keep my eyes forward, knowing my family won't be among their ranks and refusing to let that fact damper the sheer joy of today.

All the flights are on the parade field, yet, despite the sheer number of cadets, the massive field still manages to dwarf us. As the ceremony kicks off, we're told to look up at the sky for a flyby of three F-15s. For the briefest of moments, out on that sun-bleached field, I allow myself to close my eyes and listen to the roar of those engines. It's breathtaking, and it takes everything I have not to burst out in a smile.

Someday.

We sing the National Anthem and raise our right hand and repeat the Honor Oath.

All thousand cadets repeat the words: *We will not lie, steal, or cheat, nor tolerate among us anyone who does. Furthermore, I resolve to do my duty and to live honorably, so help me God.* And just like when I took my Oath of Enlistment, the words get caught in my throat as their meaning fills me with pride and purpose. But this time I keep my eyes wide open, and I'm able to move through to the next event without being chastised by Jenks.

And then—as if we're just marching across a field in any drill or in any other formation on any other morning—our flights join the Cadet Wing, forming what will become our academic year squadrons.

It's hard to settle in and let myself really digest what's going on with all the pomp and circumstance around me. Not that I could grasp the magnitude of today even if I was sitting in my dorm room all by myself.

For so many weeks, today has been all about remembering the inverted-wedge formation, and when to walk here, and when to go there, and this is when you salute, and studying for the military-knowledge test, and working every morning to get my mile-and-a-half run down so I could get that Warhawk, and on and on.

Is that how it happens? How a dream becomes a reality? Crossing off items on a checklist one at a time? Maybe instead of keeping a journal like Maria, I should keep an ongoing record of every checklist I make along the way. Because if Past Carol Danvers saw today's checklist—with its *Accept Honor Graduate* and *F-15 Flyby* and *Join Cadet Wing*, she would not believe it.

Over the last thirty-seven days, I've become the person I'd always imagined.

As we march with our newly formed squadrons, I flick my gaze over the back of Maria's head. All I want to do is get her attention and then yell at the top of my lungs, *WE DID IT! THIS IS REALLY HAPPENING!*

And then I'd look back at Bianchi, Pierre, and Del Orbe to check how they're doing: Are they as proud of themselves as I am? Are they nervous and scared, or relieved and full of happiness? Or maybe all four? Or are they just trying to get their feet right and their salute right and hope they don't sweat through their blues?

As each squadron conducts their own pass and review, I am barely able to contain myself. It's our turn, and I can feel all that training and all those drills paying off, as my stride falls in with the other cadets. We salute the commandant of cadets as one unit and move past in lockstep.

The ceremony comes to an end, and we are now fourth-class cadets.

I am now Airman Danvers.

The next moments are a blur of handshakes and back slaps and pulled-in-tight hugs. Parting words of wisdom from OCs Chen and Resendiz. I search the field for Maria, but Del Orbe tackles Pierre and me in a raucous, lunging hug, all formalities forgotten in the glory of the day. There are congratulations and yawps of joy. Del Orbe drags Pierre along, and his two-man congratulations wagon moves on to the next crowd of newly minted airmen.

"Congratulations," Bianchi says, walking up.

"Congratulations to you," I say, still searching for Maria.

We are quiet.

"I was wrong," Bianchi says, his voice an eruption. I stop scanning the field and focus on him. I wait while he rests his hands on his hips and searches the grass, like he's trying to buy himself a minute. Finally he says, again, "I was wrong." He can only repeat himself.

As Bianchi stands in front of me, the picture of contrition, I feel like I just got smacked in the face.

"Oh no," I say.

"What?"

I shake my head. "I'm on the cusp of being the first baby."

"How—?"

"You made fun of me—and just now? As you were pouring your heart out—"

"I mean, I wasn't *pouring*—"

"As you were pouring your heart out, do you want to know what I was thinking?"

"Sure?" Bianchi looks legitimately terrified.

"That I couldn't wait to tell you that you were wrong. And that I won. And that"—the second realization takes my breath away—"I want to rub your nose in it." What I don't add is *just like I want to do with Jenks*. I pull the words the state trooper scrawled onto that ticket all those weeks ago out of the depths of my brain: *Let yourself learn*.

"And what do you want to say now?" Bianchi asks.

Think, Danvers. Take a breath. Let yourself learn. "I want to be a good airman," I say at last, slowly.

"Me too."

"I didn't know that in order to be a good airman, I had to be a good human." I see my words hit Bianchi like a truck. "I know that sounds cheesy or whatever."

"It doesn't." Bianchi shakes his head and looks up at me. "It doesn't sound cheesy."

"I think we're going to win more often than we lose. I thought that was going to be the hard part. The winning. But now I think the hard part is going to be making sure I don't lose my integrity . . . along the way."

"There you are!" Maria says, settling herself between Bianchi and me. We snap out of our conversation and both turn toward her.

"Congratulations, Airman Rambeau," Bianchi says to Maria. Then he clears his throat and looks around. "I'd better find Pierre and Del Orbe before they launch into the commandant of cadets for a hug." One last wave and Bianchi heads off in search of his friends.

"I figured it out," she says as soon as Bianchi is out of earshot, unable to keep from beaming.

"Figured what out? You've only been gone for like ten minutes."

"I know how we're going to get our private pilot's license," she says, her voice quivering with excitement.

My eyes widen. "Are you . . . are you serious?"

"Yeah. I have a plan, Danvers."

CHAPTER 7

MARIA AND I SPEED AWAY FROM THE USAFA campus that Sunday, a rare day off from training. The roar of my Mustang engine coming to life after so many weeks being left unused feels like recovering a piece of myself I'd forgotten in the blur of Basic. We exchange a contented, borderline-smug look as we peel off, feeling like we've gotten away with something, even though we have no idea what it could be. Then we roll down our windows and let the crisp early-morning air cleanse and awaken us as we sail down the hill toward Maria's plan.

As is always the way with exciting road-trip adventures, the glow of luminous possibilities begins to fade with every red light, every clueless meandering driver we're stuck behind, and every frustrating traffic jam that keeps us trapped and motionless, bringing us back to earth bit by bit. As Maria scans radio stations for a better song, the beginnings of another blisteringly hot summer day hits the side of my face like the blast from an open oven door.

With the adrenaline subsiding, I'm feeling something much more troubling: anxiety, mixed with a hefty dose of doubt as to what it is we're about to do here, and whether I can do it at all.

I sift through some of my emotions, trying to land on something to share that will ease this burden but that won't completely scare Maria off. I haven't had that many opportunities to have a best friend—certainly not someone as awesome as her. I don't want to alarm her with the part of my brain that's suddenly speeding ahead even faster than the Mustang, cycling through everything that could go wrong and every way that we could fail and prove our naysayers right. I shrug my shoulders as if commanding my body to relax, to appear as careless and casual as possible, and in doing so, force my insides to fall into line.

"Why are you doing that weird thing with your shoulders?" Maria asks before I utter one "carefree" word.

"I'm being breezy," I say, and Maria barks out the biggest laugh I've ever heard from her. She can't catch her breath. She actually slaps her knee at one point. "Easy, breezy." I shrug my shoulders again and she pitches forward with a lingering cackle. "That's me."

"Danvers, and this is the biggest compliment I could ever pay you, you couldn't be breezy if you spent ten years training yourself," Maria says, swiping her tears away.

"I actually did spend a year of my life training myself to be breezy!"

"What?" Maria asks, still laughing. Now my own giggles are erupting out of me like lava. I can barely contain myself as I tell my own tragic history.

"There was this girl in my fourth-grade class who would just gaze out the window of our classroom and sigh. I was fighting with my pencil to learn cursive and struggling through division, and there she was, just impenetrable. She seemed so dreamy. I spent all year trying to copy her." We stop at another red light. I perch my elbow on my steering wheel and cradle my face in my hand just so. I sweep my gaze across the windshield and, with a contented sigh, melt into my seat. I look over at Maria with a raised eyebrow.

"I mean, like everything else you put your mind

to . . . it's exceptional," Maria says, her tone mock serious. "Although, I can see your jaw clenching from here, so . . ." The light turns green and we roll through the same intersection where just a few months prior I'd had my little run-in with State Trooper Wright. I scan the mountain roads and the far-off horizon for her squad car. I don't know what I'd say to her now. Probably just . . . thank you.

"I'd just gotten sick of always being called intense, you know?"

"Intense is good," Maria says.

"Not for little girls."

"For little girls who want to be the first female fighter pilots?" Maria nods her head, and I can see her mood darken. "Intense is good." Maria looks over at me and I can see the weariness in her eyes.

"You too?"

"*She's just a lot,*" Maria says, her voice high and dripping with faux concern. "*You better break that spirit.*" We fall into silence. And before I can filter it or pretty it up, I just start talking.

"I have a hard time not doing all this just to prove them all wrong." There. I said it. Maria and I have a plan, but without that intense fire of wanting to prove myself right, and them wrong, fueling me . . . I feel like a barely flickering candle instead of a flame-thrower. Doubt is a new feeling for me, but I can't help but think: Will it be enough to just have *me* driving me through all of this? I want it to be enough. But I'm not used to doing things out of my own internal motivations.

"The twenty percent rubbing their noses in it thing," Maria says with a nod.

"Thirty percent but—"

"It's thirty percent now?" I can't look at her. Maria waits. The silence expands as a soft, ethereal-sounding voice floats from the radio, raspy and beautiful.

"Okay, yes. The percentage is climbing. And yes, I'm worried that pretty soon that percentage will go all the way up to one hundred, and like I've done my entire life, I'll be doing something just to prove everyone else wrong. And that's no way to live. And yes, I've heard the saying 'Do you want to be right or do you want to be happy,' but look, why not be both right *and* happy? Huh? Ever think of that?" As Maria shakes her head and laughs, I turn into the driveway she's circled on her map for us, and proceed down the long dusty road.

"You gotta get out of your head, Danvers. It's pretty scary in there. Ooh, look, I think this is it—it should be right over there," she says, craning her neck and searching the vast expanse of land ahead.

And then, I feel it. The low growl of its engine vibrates throughout the Mustang, its singsongy hum snaking up my spine just like it always used to when I spent my days craning my neck toward the skies instead of grinding through training courses on the ground. I slow the car, and Maria and I look up—in back of us, overhead, off on the horizon.

"It feels like it's in the car with us," Maria says, now almost completely hanging out of the passenger window to get a better look. The growl and purr grow closer. I pull into a parking spot just next to hangar thirty-nine, and Maria and I leap out of the car just in time to see that same yellow biplane with the blue and red accents, the only one I couldn't name on my first morning in Colorado, soar overhead, lining up with its runway and touching down.

"It's wonderful," I say, smiling wide and unguarded. I look over at Maria and her face is just as open and just as joyous.

"Beautiful," Maria says, in a glorious daze. And without a word or any agreement, both of us take off running toward the plane as it rumbles on to hangar thirty-nine.

The plane approaches us as we try to balance ogling it with not getting run over. As it gets closer, I notice two open cockpits—one behind the other. Maria and I watch and wait as the two pilots guide the plane into the hangar and finally shut the plane down with a last shudder. We can barely contain ourselves.

The pilot in the front climbs down first and stands on the wing. Then he and another man who's emerged from the hangar help the other pilot to climb out of his cockpit. Both pilots hop down, and the one in the front takes off his bomber hat and goggles.

Maria and I can't help but look at each other with a now almost atomic level of excitement. *He* is a *she*. The other pilot takes off his bomber hat and goggles—this one is unmistakably male—and they both make their way over to us.

"You look just like your dad," the man says to Maria. His salt-and-pepper hair is closely cropped, and the indentation of the goggles has left an imprint on his wind-burned russet skin. His face is lined with age but still maintains a sense of youth. Open, yet cryptic. It seems the pilot is just as inscrutable as the plane.

"You've gotten so big," the woman says, just before

pulling Maria in for a hug. Her voice is a wobbly rasp. Her light brown hair is mussed from the bomber hat, and just like the man beside her, the goggles have left a mark on her tawny-beige skin—which only calls more attention to her huge hazel eyes. She's the most quietly powerful woman I've ever met.

"Carol Danvers, this is Jack and Bonnie Thompson. They flew with my dad," Maria says, absolutely beaming with pride and adoration. Both Jack and Bonnie extend their hands to me, and I find myself completely speechless.

"It's . . . wow . . . I . . . It's nice to meet you," I finally manage. And then I can no longer hold it in: "If I could? Please . . . what kind of plane is that?"

"*Mr. Goodnight?*" Jack asks.

I laugh. "Why'd you name the plane *Mr. Goodnight*?" I ask.

"You'll see when you fly him," Jack says, with a wink.

"When I fly him?"

"It's a 1942 Stearman. PT-Seventeen," Bonnie cuts in.

"It's what I trained in," Jack adds.

"And so will you," Bonnie says with a wry smile. Maria and I share a look of deep concern. The plane is magnificent in its own way, but it's not what either of us had envisioned earning our forty hours of flight training with.

"Not quite the plane you guys were imagining for this little flying school Maria here has arranged?" Jack asks, reading my mind as he leads us toward the hangar.

We enter, and any misgivings I had disappear. Hangar thirty-nine is what I envision heaven would look like.

Dimly lit and cool, it's bigger than any building should be. In one shadowy corner there's a beautiful, pristine T-41 Mescalero. And lurking in the wayback, Jack and Bonnie have—no biggie—a couple of civilian Cessnas. There's that P-51D Mustang I heard—its engine now deconstructed and laid out on the floor. Tools, engine parts, cleaning supplies, and propellers are scattered under an old World War II poster of Captain America saluting us good citizens for buying war bonds. The entire space is controlled chaos, and it's wonderful. Jack switches on an old radio perched precariously atop their workbench, and the crack of a baseball bat bursts through the cavernous space as some far-off radio announcer calls a game.

"So, Maria tells us you want to get your private pilot's license so you can join the Flying Falcons?" Bonnie asks, setting up an old coffeemaker. Jack reaches up to a higher shelf and hands Bonnie a can of coffee, along with a stack of filters. She thanks him just as he winces, reacting to a less-than-stellar development in his baseball game.

"Yes, ma'am . . . Pilot Thom . . . Mrs. Thom—" I stumble.

"Just Bonnie, honey." She makes eye contact. "You can just call me Bonnie."

I nod and try again. "Bonnie." She smiles at me and I melt.

"Bonnie flew transports in the war," Maria says.

"Trained me to fly," Jack adds.

"I wanted to fly combat, but . . ." Bonnie trails off. She doesn't have to finish. We know.

"So do we," Maria says.

"And you think getting into the Flying Falcons will . . . what?" Bonnie asks, the smell of percolating coffee now wafting throughout the hangar. Maria and I look at each other. We know what this sounds like when we say it out loud. Especially to Bonnie.

"Change their minds," I say, trying to sound as sure as possible. Maria nods in agreement.

"We both got the Warhawk, and we're both Honor Graduates. We were on the Honor Squadron. And by the time Recognition comes around at the end of the year, we want to add the Flying Falcons to that list," Maria says.

"So these are tryouts for next year's team?" Jack asks. Maria and I nod.

"You know you're going to have to work twice as hard to get half as much," Bonnie says, making particularly pointed eye contact with Maria.

"I've been doing that my whole life," Maria says resolutely.

"I know you have," Bonnie says. Jack puts his arm around Bonnie's waist.

There's a lull, and I know it's because Jack and Bonnie are deciding whether or not to try and talk us out of our plan. They'll say that getting into the Flying Falcons won't change anyone's minds. That female pilots have been wanting to fly combat since Bonnie's generation begged for the opportunity decades ago. That this quest of ours has to be worthy and valuable even if we don't get what we want in the end.

I know they'd be right. But I also know that everyone in this hangar is all too familiar with what it's like to be denied something they've earned.

Jack's and Bonnie's eyes meet, and they share a grin.

"Then let's get started," Jack says, clapping his hands together.

"All right!" I cheer. Maria and I high-five and turn to walk back out to the Stearman.

"Where are you two going?" Jack's voice comes from behind us.

We slowly turn back. "To the plane?" Maria says, as if she's stating the obvious. Bonnie allows a winsome smile and makes her way back to the coffeemaker.

"We're not going to be getting you up in the air quite yet," Jack says.

"But—"

"You'll get your forty hours before the tryouts, but first we need to build some of that character and integrity," Jack says.

"And how are, um, *we* going to do that?" Maria asks. I can hear the trepidation in her voice.

"Just under that poster of Cap?" Jack says, pointing over his shoulder. Maria and I both nod. "There's a bucket full of cleaning supplies and some old rags. Take those, fill the bucket with water, and give *Mr. Goodnight* a nice once-over, if you don't mind." Bonnie walks back over and hands Jack a mug of coffee. "Thank you, sweetheart."

"I thought we were going to fly?" I ask.

"Character and integrity first." Jack takes a sip of his coffee. "Then you fly."

CHAPTER 8

"WE REEK," I COMPLAIN HOURS LATER, AS WE drive back to campus that evening under the dusk of a setting sun. "Who knew getting something clean could get you so *dirty*?"

Maria hums with agreement, but as I navigate us home it's clear we're both happy with how the day turned out, unexpected as it was. With every centimeter of *Mr. Goodnight* that we cleaned, Jack and Bonnie were right there to tell us what that part did and how it worked. *This dial is connected to this in the engine that does this, and if that doesn't work, well, you can pull this or do that, and see how it all works together just like that?*

I couldn't quite see it yet, but after just a few hours

under their careful tutelage it became clear that I'd learn to.

I'd always pictured myself in a cockpit, soaring through the clouds. I could see that with perfect clarity. But when I actually tried to imagine how all those baby steps would feel, I could never do it. In the end, the best I could muster up was some feel-good dreams where I doled out endless hang-loose signs after I'd done something awe-inspiring with seemingly zero effort and the gracefulness of a swan.

But today, as I was bending over *Mr. Goodnight*'s engine, sleeves rolled up and covered in grease and oil, taking the tiniest of baby steps toward my ultimate goal, I felt wonderment. And a hunger for more. And pride. I felt happy. I felt like I belonged. When I looked over at Jack as he took apart a piece of *Mr. Goodnight*'s engine and started explaining what each and every part of it did, it felt like I had stepped into the other half of my puzzle piece. Which is probably why I couldn't imagine it before today. I had no idea this sort of self-completion was even possible, let alone how it would feel. It was just easier to imagine soaring through the skies and letting others be amazed by me, rather than imagine what it would feel like to be amazed by myself.

Once we make our way back, shower, and settle into our room for the night, though, my brain lifts from the glorious fog of Stearman engine parts and crashes back down to preparing for our first day of school tomorrow.

"This is going to be killer," Maria mutters as we examine our printed schedules before turning out the lights. We're expected to take four classes in the morning and three in the afternoon, play on an intramural team, and take Introduction to Soaring, the first class in the airmanship program. We've already checked in with Bianchi, Del Orbe, and Pierre about setting up nightly study groups in McDermott Library so we can all keep each other from getting too overwhelmed, but the workload seems insanely intense.

I toss and turn all night, building elaborate houses of cards from *what-ifs* or possible scenarios for the next day. When Maria and I start lacing up our sneakers for our morning run at our usual early hour, I'm already operating on pure adrenaline and actively avoiding any more emotional trapdoors.

We walk onto the track to find Bianchi, Del Orbe, and Pierre already stretching. I can hear Del Orbe's laugh from the other side of the field.

"Do y'all know what Flickerball is?" Pierre asks as soon as we're within earshot.

"It's pretty much just half football and half dodge-ball," Maria says, bending over and touching her toes with a sleepy groan.

"In my brain right now is a slideshow of people getting hit in the face with a ball and then someone standing over them yelling *that's Flickerball!*" Pierre says. He sounds slightly hysterical, his voice rising at an uneven pitch.

"Yeah, that's about right," Bianchi says with a laugh.

"You guys got Flickerball?" I ask Bianchi as Del Orbe reenacts Pierre's grisly version of the game.

"We all did. You?" He asks.

"Us too," I say, answering for Maria. Bianchi nods.

"So, our intramural sport for the entire year is just basically my junior high school nightmare," Pierre says. "That's great. Just great. Fantastic, really!"

"Pierre, relax," Maria says, ever the voice of calm and reason. "You guys ready?" she asks, hopping high into the air over and over. Everyone begrudgingly nods, and we set off around the track as a group.

"Where'd you guys get off to yesterday?" Bianchi asks, keeping pace with me in the front of the pack.

"Wouldn't you like to know," I retort.

"Yes, that's customarily why people ask questions. Because they would like to know."

I laugh, and his face softens.

"Would it make it weird if I didn't tell you just yet?" I ask.

"Of course not." But a sidelong glance confirms I've confused him. "Sorry if I overstepped, Danvers."

"No, it's okay. I just don't want to jinx it."

"But it's very cool, and you're going to be *so* jealous," Maria coos as she glides past us.

Bianchi and I grow quiet as we round the track.

"You *are* going to tell me though, right?" he finally asks.

"Maybe," I say. He arches an eyebrow. "Yes, okay? I promise."

"And not like on my deathbed or something, just in case you're looking for a loophole," he says.

"How dare you, sir," I call over my shoulder, picking up the pace to catch up with Maria. "I am an honest and stalwart lady."

"I know you are," Bianchi says, his voice momentarily serious. I smile and catch up to Maria, leaving Bianchi behind.

"You could have told him," Maria says, her breath puffing in the brisk morning air.

"I just want to keep it ours a bit longer," I say, not

knowing where that decision has come from, but somehow intuiting that it feels right. Maria nods and we fall into a happy, peaceful syncopation around the track.

In the past, I would have blurted out what we were doing to show off or impress someone . . . *anyone. You may not think much of me, but you must surely be dazzled with this super-fancy thing I'm accomplishing that you aren't. Ta-daaaaaa!*

But now? There's something almost sacred about hangar thirty-nine. Something I don't want to sully with all those past insecurities. I want to tell people about it for the right reasons, not so I can feel remarkable for a few fleeting moments. I'm proud of myself, not just because I have something new and shiny to parade around. I smirk at my thought process—as if cleaning a Stearman to within an inch of itself is something others would even be jealous of.

By 5:00 a.m., we're dripping in sweat and heading back to the dorms in search of a much-needed shower. Bianchi, Pierre, and Del Orbe peel off as Maria and I weave our way through the hallways. Then we notice Noble coming back from a run of her own. With no Johnson in sight, I decide to extend a bit of an olive branch as we climb the stairs.

"I don't think we've officially met, by the way. I'm

Carol, and that's Maria," I say, inclining my head in Maria's direction.

"I'm Noble," she says, her voice an acerbic drawl. Her fire-red hair is pulled back in a tight bun, and her freckled pale skin is flushed from her morning exercise. Her deep green eyes always seem to be at a too-cool half-mast.

"I was hoping for a first name," I say jokingly, but also meaning it at the same time. This has to be a give-and-take, or we'll be nowhere.

Noble sighs the longest, weariest sigh in the history of sighs. My curiosity has apparently exhausted her. I plaster a breezy smile on my face through sheer grit. I can hear Maria stifle a giggle just behind me.

"Zoë," she says.

"Hey, Zoë," Maria says with a flick of her head. Zoë nods toward her in cool reply.

"So I'll see you guys when I see you, I guess," Zoë says, sidling down the hall and disappearing into her dorm room.

"Great!" I flap my hand enthusiastically after her retreating form, the complete opposite of Maria and Zoë's effortless, distant cool.

"Was that a wave, Danvers?" Maria says, barely able to contain herself.

"She's too cool for me," I say, opening up the door to our own room and gathering my stuff for the showers. I hear Maria's cackle follow me all the way down the hallway.

But by 7:30 a.m., it doesn't matter who's cool and who isn't, who commands a reaction with a lift of her perfectly arched eyebrow and who exercises all the restraint of a bull in a china shop, because collected and awkward, confident and terrified alike, we're all sitting in our very first lessons as fourth-class cadets at the United States Air Force Academy.

CHAPTER 9

"**W**ELCOME TO INTRODUCTION TO SOARING. I'M Captain Jenks."

Ugh.

Captain Jenks paces in front of us as he speaks, his hands clasped behind him. His aviator sunglasses glint and shimmer in the sunlight, obscuring his all-knowing gaze as he waxes rhapsodic about his expectations for us during our time in his class. The cadet instructor pilots stand behind him, steely and unmoving, as planes take off and land on the bustling runways just beyond.

"Throughout the year you will go on four hops, always accompanied by an instructor. You will not fly solo until you are a third-class cadet." The loud rumble of a taxiing tow plane drowns out the last of Captain Jenks's words, but his meaning is clear.

I turn around and see a tow plane pulling one of the gliders from behind a large hangar. The glider looks more like a motorcycle sidecar, clunky and rounded in the front with red piping that traces its lean fuselage and loops around the words STARK INDUSTRIES, emblazoned on the fin of the plane. The glider is all wing, its design mind-bogglingly—and quite exhilaratingly—simple.

I can't wait to fly her.

Captain Jenks tells us that we'll each be paired with one of the cadet instructor pilots. I scan the options and immediately rank them from most to least favorite, based mainly on super-scientific methods like how they're standing and the set of their jaws. I should be more embarrassed that someone who would very much like for people to stop judging her book by its cover has just jumped to wild conclusions about a group of people's characters and teaching abilities based on nothing but appearances. Yet, here we are.

"Danvers, you're with Cadet Instructor Pilot Wolff," Jenks says as he goes down the list without glancing my way.

I groan inwardly. For the record, I'd already labeled Cadet Instructor Pilot Wolff as my least favorite. Tall and sturdy, square jawed and arrogant, Wolff looks like he's hung more than a few *kick me* signs on people in his day.

I don't know any of the airmen in my group under Cadet Instructor Pilot Wolff. I glare over at Maria and Del Orbe. I'm envious that they were grouped together with my first choice, Cadet Instructor Pilot Cabot, he of the mellow face and relaxed posture. They don't notice my glare, of course, because they're now blissfully frolicking through the airfield hand in hand with my first choice, while I prepare myself to get the mental wedgie of a lifetime.

"Let's get started," Wolff says. His voice is low and methodical. Our group follows him like little ducklings over to the glider.

"Hop in," he says to me.

"Sir?" I ask, looking at the three other airmen in my group, thinking both that this offer is some kind of trap, and feeling discomfort at having to go first. Wolff says nothing. His light brown hair rustles in the wind, his ruddy skin already looking in need of a shave despite the razor that certainly scraped his face first thing this morning. His coal-black eyes are piercing, and his ability to hold a silence is herculean.

I nod and climb into the cockpit of a plane for the very first time.

And inside my body I feel a *click* as all the pieces of my life resolutely, assuredly fall into place.

I take a deep breath and securely strap in, trying to swallow my erupting emotions. I curl my fingers around the glider's stick, and scan the plane's instruments. Instruments that are right here in front of me and not pictured in some dog-eared, worn-out airplane magazine I found in the waiting room of the garage where I used to get my car fixed.

If cleaning the Stearman felt like a gift, sitting in this cockpit is nothing short of an answered prayer.

I did it. This is real. I'm here.

I fight the urge to give Wolff a thumbs-up, and instead brush my fingers over the compass, looping over the altimeter. I tap on the airspeed indicator and then crane my head back to catch a glimpse of the tiny yaw string attached to the canopy. A humble piece of yarn, also used by the Wright Brothers, that's stood the test of time as the best method to make sure an aircraft is flying as efficiently as possible and not listing sideways. I smile wide as I find it, marveling at the timelessness of a simple good idea.

"Tell us what you see," Wolff commands. I fight every urge to blurt, *My dreams coming true!*

"Power," I say instead.

"That's good, Danvers." Wolff turns away from me and faces the three other airmen. He takes a long, thoughtful pause, and we all hang on his every breath, dissecting each time he clenches and unclenches his jaw. Finally, "In this plane, you will feel every capricious whim the sky has in store for you." Wolff turns back to me. "You must be prepared for every possibility."

"Restraint," Jenks says, coming up behind Wolff.

"Sir?" Wolff asks.

"To answer your question, 'What do you see?'" Jenks circles the glider, his hands clasped behind his back, his thumb twitching with every step.

"Yes, sir," Wolff says.

"It is usually in the cockpit where one first learns one's limitations."

"And one's liberation," Wolff adds. The silence expands. Wolff lets it. "Sir."

"Soaring is mastered by those who practice control and self-discipline. It is not for the impulsive, the careless, or the emotional," Jenks says. Each word knocks the wind out of me, feeling like a personal attack.

"In the impulsive, we find the passionate. In the careless, we find the bold. And in the emotional, we find the human. What's important, sir, is if they can be taught." Wolff stands between Jenks and me, and I decide I was wholly mistaken in labeling him my least favorite cadet instructor pilot.

"Well. I shall be very interested to see how your little experiment"—Jenks trails off, dragging his gaze over me as if I were a musty, wet towel—"ends."

"Yes, sir."

Jenks scans the other three airmen, pushes his shoulders back, and wordlessly walks over to another group. Wolff taps the side of the plane, and I take that to mean that I should hop out. None of us speak of what just happened, but as I climb from the glider I am bathing in it. I am also seething. How dare Jenks try to color my first cockpit experience with his unyielding, cold words?

I tighten my fist and instead try to remember what the glider's stick felt like in my hand. What it felt like to sit in the cockpit. The *click* that no one, not even Jenks, can take away from me. I belong here. This is what I was made to do, however impulsive, careless, and emotional I may sometimes be. I finally inhale a deep breath and Jenks's words begin to evaporate, droplet by droplet.

I stand aside and watch as the other three airmen sit in the cockpit and get some piece of sage advice from Wolff, whose esteem grows in my eyes every additional moment we spend together. He may look like a high school jock, but underneath all that swagger he's just another kid who's always dreamed of flying.

We spend the rest of our time going over the basics, paying rapt attention to every tidbit Wolff thoughtfully—and ever so slowly—imparts to us. By the end of our time together, I am in awe. How must it feel to be so confident as to take up as much time and space as Wolff? To not allow oneself to be moved.

I am lost in thought as I glide through the rest of the day, sitting through classes even while my brain lingers resolutely on every curve of that glider, what it felt like to be belted in, and what the world looked like from inside a cockpit. As I file away every sensation to be savored later, there's one thing I can't seem to corral into just one image or moment. It's part of the same lesson that's been fluttering around me for the past few months.

Deep down, I've always known that I belonged in the cockpit of a plane. I just automatically thought that in order to make that true, someone else—someone truly important (unlike me)—would need to give me their stamp of approval. Which is why someone like Jenks's respect means so much to me. Sure, when I sat in that cockpit today I felt more myself, more at peace, and more perfectly made for something than I ever have before, but a part of me still wouldn't—couldn't—call it truth or fact until Jenks gave me his expert opinion.

But watching Wolff be so sure of himself, trusting his own gut feeling enough to challenge Jenks, I'm realizing that all this time, it's been easier to depend on someone else's approval of me, someone who holds a position of power and importance, than to approve of myself. Or, to take it even further, to demand that others approve of me whether they like it or not.

Let yourself learn. State Trooper Wright's words pinball around my head, and before these additional meanings they've now taken on can vaporize, I pluck them up and pin them to a bulletin board in my brain.

My brain is throbbing by the time Maria and I settle

in at McDermott Library for our study session that evening. Bianchi, Del Orbe, and Pierre trickle in, and slowly but surely our table is overrun with books and sheets upon sheets of scribbled notes, all this mass of knowledge after just one day of classes.

Noble sits at the next table over. We—okay, I—ask her if she wants to join us, but she politely (or at least with her version of politeness) declines. Her mouth does quirk up on one side in an approximation of a smile, though, so I'd say she's coming around.

"Did your soaring instructor tell you about the air show?" Maria whispers in between assignments.

"No, what air show?" I ask, looking up from my notes.

"I guess everyone in the airmanship program gets to go to an air show," Maria says. I wait expectantly for more, but there's only silence. She laughs. "Sounded like I had way more to say about it, didn't it?"

"It totally did," I say, laughing.

"The Thunderbirds are going to be there," Bianchi puts in. The Thunderbirds are basically the Flying Falcons times a million.

"I heard they might be flying the brand-new F-Sixteens instead of those old T-thirty-eights," Del Orbe says.

"Hey, now. Those Talons were cool," Pierre says. And everyone stops. "I saw them at Robins down in Georgia. My family drove for hours to watch them and . . ." Pierre trails off into a dreamy world we all know far too well.

"Jenks used to be a Thunderbird," Noble says from the next table. We all look over. She's slumped over her stacks of books, pencil still tight in her hand.

"What?" I ask.

"Did he retire?" Bianchi asks.

"I heard he got grounded," Noble says, her voice a lethargic exhale, lowered so that we're all leaning forward to better hear this piece of information on the inimitable Jenks.

"Do you know why?" I ask.

"If I knew why, I would have said, 'I heard he got grounded because of this reason,' now wouldn't I?" Noble says, sliding her gaze away from us and back down to her books.

"Well. You are a delight," Del Orbe says.

"Aw, thank you. Thank you so much," Noble says, her tone dripping in sarcasm. So much for coming around.

"How could someone get grounded from the Thunderbirds?" I ask, turning back to our little huddle.

"Danvers," Maria warns. Her tone is serious. So serious that it makes Del Orbe, Pierre, and Bianchi dive back into their studies so Maria and I can, apparently, have a private moment.

I lift my hands in a gesture of surrender. "What? Don't you think this is at least a little bit interesting? Don't you—?"

"I need you to loosen your stubborn grip as you try to figure out whatever happened in this man's past." Maria's eyes are locked onto mine as she interrupts me.

"But—"

"Or are you thinking of raising that number to forty percent after all? Find out his weak spot and stick it to him, maybe, as a bonus?"

My face colors. Maria knows me better than I'd even thought. "Forty percent is not even half, by the way," I grumble, unable to put up any kind of fight.

"The only reason Jenks has any power over you is because you keep giving it to him," Maria says.

"Ouch," I say, her words hitting me right between the eyes.

"Promise me, Danvers." Maria doesn't break our gaze. "Promise me you'll leave it." I can see Del Orbe, Pierre, and Bianchi trying not to eavesdrop. But as I take my time in promising Maria that I'll leave it alone, I can hear Bianchi whisper, "Come on, Danvers," under his breath.

"I promise," I say.

CHAPTER 10

"WAIT, WHAT'S THE AIR HORN FOR?" I YELL AT Jack over the sound of *Mr. Goodnight*'s engine. The entire plane is rumbling and shaking as I belt myself into the open front cockpit. I tuck the air horn in tight next to me.

"To communicate with," Jack yells back.

"There's no radio?" I ask, clicking my belts into place. Maria and Bonnie wave, excitedly falling back into conversation, going over their first hop.

"I can talk to you, but you can't talk to me," Jack says.

"Yes, sir!" I yell, trying to make my reply as brief and not-scared as possible.

"One for vomit and two for crashing," Jack says. I look down at the horn.

"One for vomit and two for crashing," I repeat, nodding. I'd hate to mix those two up.

After weeks of ground lessons with Jack and Bonnie, it's finally time to fly. Bonnie and Maria just returned from the air, Maria's face aglow; now it's my turn, with Jack at the helm.

"Put your hands on the instruments, Danvers," Jack yells. My throttle moves as Jack taxis the plane away from hangar thirty-nine. That's the beauty of these old training planes that I've come to appreciate, despite the initial shock of being trained on the Stearman as opposed to something new and shiny. All the instruments in my cockpit are mirrored in Jack's. So I experience what he's doing, and I learn, in real time, how to fly. I curl my fingers around the throttle, and the sensation around my entire body is like fireworks.

"You got your feet on the rudders?" he calls to me. I holler in the affirmative as I stretch out my legs and place them on the rudders of the old plane.

The plane's violent shaking threatens to dislodge the air horn, so I quickly shove it under my leg as tightly as I can. The propeller spins and spins, finally going so fast that it looks like it's not spinning at all. At first I thought the excitement would eclipse all my education and I wouldn't be able to keep my head in all this. But it's the exact opposite. I've never been so laser-focused in my whole life. Every sound, every feeling, every scan of the instruments locks me more and more into a groove.

I was made for this.

I hear Jack through the radio, talking to the tower. Requesting clearance and repeating a series of numbers as we rumble closer and closer to the runway. Our plane idles at the end of the strip and I can feel every cell of my body alive and ready. That haunting singsongy hum of *Mr. Goodnight*'s engine snakes up my spine. That growl and purr, which was once was so far and mystifyingly above me, now envelops me like an old friend's caress.

And then, Jack taxis *Mr. Goodnight* onto the runway. We begin to speed up faster and faster and faster, and all I can hear is the wind and that powerful engine, and I feel the shaking beneath us, and then with one stomach-dropping swoop—

No more shaking.

We. Are. Flying.

As we leave the ground, my heart feels as though it might explode out of my chest. Jack's firm, gentle hand eases us higher and higher. The impossibly blue sky is no longer way up there, unattainable. It surrounds me. I'm up here, too. I laugh. I can't help it. It's everything I thought it would be. It's everything I wished it would be. It's everything I knew it would be. And more. So much more.

Jack banks us left, and the world below opens up underneath us: green and brown and mountains and fields and tiny dots of people going about their day. We straighten out and climb higher still.

When Jack hits cruising speed at just over one hundred miles per hour, I feel us settle into the blue just like any other bird soaring on the ebbs and flows of the airstream.

"You ready to take him, Danvers?" Jack asks, crackling through the radio.

"Yes, sir!" I scream. I've never been more ready in my life.

My whole body tightens and relaxes all at once. A deep breath and I can feel Jack let go, as the throttle becomes mine and mine alone.

I turn the throttle left, easing it over, and watch as *Mr. Goodnight's* wings dip low into the sky, listening to me, following what I do.

"I DID THAT!" I yell into the sky.

Jack cautions me through the motions as I bring the

plane back to level, his voice a soothing presence in my ear that keeps me from getting too carried away. Right turns are a bit trickier, so I'm especially focused on Jack's instructions for navigating the delicate balance of throttle pressure and rudders. But soon enough, I've got *Mr. Goodnight* banking right with ease.

"All right, Danvers. No need to show off." He chuckles through the radio.

"This is amazing!" I yell to no one in particular, just needing to hear myself to know this is all really happening. As Jack and I fly and practice turning and leveling and climbing and *right turn here* and *left turn there*, I have no nagging thoughts left about needing to prove myself to others, about doing this to show everyone who ever doubted me that they were wrong. My brain is here in this cockpit and nowhere else.

Before I know it, it's time to take *Mr. Goodnight* home.

I scan the horizon and realize I have no idea where home is.

"Give him back to me, and I'll take us home," Jack says, as though reading my thoughts, his voice crackling through the radio. The throttle moves and the plane sweeps across the sky with an ease that makes me tear up. Just the right angle, just the right pressure.

Suddenly my swoops and turns feel clunky, graceless, in comparison. Jack is an artist.

You'll get there, too, one day, I tell myself.

As Jack talks to the tower, I finally see the airport's hangars and runways dappling the landscape in front of us. I scan the horizon for any other planes and see nothing but blue sky.

"Pay close attention to this landing, Danvers," Jack says through the radio. I watch as Jack lines up *Mr. Goodnight* with the runway just next to hangar thirty-nine. The ground closes in, rushing up to meet us, and as I hold my breath, Jack sets all three of the plane's tires down in one seamless motion, without even a single bounce.

"That was beautiful!" I yell. I can hear Jack's rumbling, smoky laugh behind me. And as we taxi *Mr. Goodnight* toward hangar thirty-nine, I use the loud rumbling engine to mask an eruption of laughing and yelling and trembling and everything that I felt up in the air.

I think back to that yaw string on the glider. A simple piece of yarn that keeps the pilot from slipping or skidding one way or the other. I think about how Jack and Wolff and even Maria each seem to have their own internal yaw string. An intrinsic piece of yarn that keeps them steady no matter how hard the wind tries to blow them off course. They are their own expert opinions. They are their own yaw strings. I want to have that, and today feels like it's as close as I've gotten to obtaining it in my entire life.

Joy explodes out of my every pore, voluminous enough to take us back up into the sky even without engine power. Is this what I'm trying to temper by obsessing about Jenks? Do I direct all my energy toward proving myself because somewhere deep inside I fear the freedom I felt up there in the sky? And the power. The power I keep giving to people like Jenks.

Why am I so afraid of my own power?

Why is he?

I hop down from the plane and run over to Maria, lunging into her for a hug. She wraps her arms tight around me and we both know there are no words for what we experienced and felt up there today. We've been completed.

We cling to each other. Neither of us are big huggers, but it's like we both know that if there was ever a time for a hug, now is it.

"How'd she do?" Bonnie asks Jack as he sidles over to join the rest of us. Maria and I finally break apart, both of us still beaming from ear to ear.

"Oh, she's brilliant," Jack says with a shrug. "Just like this one." Bonnie gazes proudly over at Maria.

"I told Maria that by the end of this she's going to do a slow barrel roll. We're going to get you to have a little fun," Bonnie says. Maria's face lights up.

"I have plans for this one, too. Not quite as fun as a barrel roll, though," Jack's eyes twinkle as his gaze meets mine.

"Jack," Bonnie warns.

"Nothing big, just maybe a teeny, itsy-bitsy, tiny power-off stall is all," Jack says.

"What's a power-off stall?" I ask, not liking any of those words. Maria's slow barrel roll sounds far preferable.

"It's a way to teach you that even if you're the best pilot in the world, sometimes things go wrong." He laughs at my face, which must look as though I've just swallowed a lemon. "Now come on. Enough about that. Let's celebrate today. Bonnie made cherry pie," Jack says, taking Bonnie by the hand and walking them into the hangar.

"Best day ever?" I ask Maria as we follow in behind them.

Her smile lights up her entire face. "Best day ever."

CHAPTER 11

"THAT'S FLICKERBALL!" I HEAR DEL ORBE YELL as Pierre lies groaning on the ground in front of him.

I laugh and look across the pitch to see Bianchi trotting toward me on the sidelines. I pick up my sweatshirt, slide it over my head, and pull my tired, sweaty arms through, already chilled even as the beads of sweat cool on my body. We've gone from fall into the beginnings of winter, and now at our early-morning runs it looks like someone has dared us to run around the track while wearing every item of clothing in our closet.

As challenging and fulfilling as these past few months have been, it still feels like everything else but the flying is all happening to someone else, real but not real. The study sessions, the classes, the afternoons spent on the Flickerball field. Walking through the hallways with held breath, taking tests with my chest tightened up, listening to lectures as my oxygen depletes—waiting for the moment I can draw in that exquisite gulp of fresh air that comes when I get to fly again. Stitching together a perfectly tolerable existence, until I can feel that stomach-dropping swoop as I'm finally able to gasp for air. Flying is my new reality, and nothing else measures up.

"Del Orbe did that to him on purpose," I say as Bianchi settles in next to me.

"He's been planning it for months," Bianchi agrees, laughing. We fall silent as we watch our team practice for next week's game. Our intramural Flickerball team is currently tied for first place, and just like Field Day, it's Johnson and Noble's squadron that we again find ourselves in contention with. This time, however, they've come way closer than any of us is comfortable with. So there's a lot riding on next week.

"You going to the air show this weekend?" I ask.

"Yeah. You?"

"Yeah."

Silence.

"Good."

Silence.

"Maria and I have been taking flying lessons at an airport just outside town so we can earn our private pilot's licenses and try out for the Flying Falcons," I say in a rush. Blurt, more like.

I can't meet Bianchi's eyes even though I can sense them on me, laser-focused. "Wait, what?"

"Well, it's never just you and me, so I can never seem to tell just you, and I didn't want to pass you some weird, mysterious note in McDermott, but I also didn't want to wait until you were on your deathbed, but it was looking like it was about to be—I mean it's been how many months since you first asked us where we go when we leave campus?"

He pauses to mull this over. "Three and a half, really almost four."

"Wow. . . . Really?" Bianchi nods, his deep blue eyes now locked onto mine. "I was going to say maybe one-ish."

"Yeah, no."

"Well, time has certainly *flown* by, har-har," I say, clearing my throat.

"So, am I allowed to ask some follow-up questions?"

Across the field Maria shoots and scores. A high five to
Pierre. A high five to Del Orbe.

"Of course," I say, giving Maria an enthusiastic
thumbs-up from the sidelines.

"Who are you taking these lessons from?"

"Jack and Bonnie Thompson. They flew with Maria's
pop in the war. Well, wars," I say, following Maria's
progress as she snakes and weaves her way through the
field. Passing. Catching. And scoring again. Bianchi
and I both clap.

"Maria's dad flew in the war?"

"He was a Tuskegee Airman," I say.

"Wow."

"So was Jack."

"And Bonnie?"

"She taught them both how to fly, and then the Air
Force let her fly transports." I can't look at him. "She
always says how proud she was to serve her country,
but . . ." I trail off. I can't say it. Bianchi nods. He takes
a deep breath and clasps his hands behind his head.
He looks down at the ground, and I can see his swirl
of breath exhale out into the cold, wintry air. When he
finally speaks, his voice is painfully kind, and I almost
wish it wasn't.

"So, this is about being able to fly combat."

"Everything is about being able to fly combat." My words are fast and violent, almost a snarl, shocking even me. "Oh god, I'm sorry. I'm so . . . Wow, I . . . I guess I am not as okay with that as I thought I was."

"I can't even begin to understand," he says. I look over at him. The field erupts into cheers as Pierre is hoisted onto the team's shoulders after his first-ever score. Bianchi and I absently applaud our friend who finally, after several painful months, is mastering Flickerball.

"I don't think I can either," I say, unable to keep from laughing as I'm continually surprised by the vacillation of my own emotions.

"What do they have you flying?" Bianchi asks, trying to lighten the mood.

"A 1942 Stearman PT-Seventeen," I say.

"What?"

"Named *Mr. Goodnight*."

"You have got to be kidding me."

"It's what Jack trained on, so it's what he's training us on," I say.

"I can't believe you've kept this to yourself," he says.

"If I told you about the flying lessons, then I'd have to tell you why we were taking them, and if I told you why we were taking them, then I would have to tell you the plan, and after I told you the plan, I'd have to stand here and watch as you chose not to tell me that the plan might not work because you didn't want to hurt my feelings."

"And what exactly is the plan?"

"Maria and I earn our private pilot's licenses and are able to try out for the Flying Falcons. We nail the tryout and maybe Jenks is brought to tears by our brilliance, I don't know, I haven't worked that part out yet. Maybe there's a tight-lipped handshake and through gritted teeth he grudgingly says, 'I was wrong about you, Danvers.' Maybe he says I'm the best flier he's ever seen and presents me with a trophy out of nowhere. I don't know—that part of the plan has become rather elaborate over the past few months." Bianchi laughs. "But then Maria and I make the Flying Falcons!" I shrug. "And they'll have to see. They'll have to see all that we've achieved this year—the Warhawk, the Honor Graduate, the Honor Squadron—and change their minds, and Maria and I will be the first female fighter pilots in the United States Air Force." I look up at him. "We're the best, Tom."

"I know you are," he says.

"Then it has to work," I say, my voice full of false bravado.

Bianchi takes a deep breath. "Just because you're the best, Carol, doesn't mean—"

"Don't say it," I say, grabbing his wrist. I don't know why I did that. It's like I have to hold him, make him stop, even as he's speaking a truth that my own mind reminds me of twenty times a day. Bianchi looks at me. "I know, okay? I know."

"Okay," he says.

I nod my thanks. In the silence that follows, I peel my fingers from around his arm.

"I still can't believe you can fly a Stearman PT-Seventeen," Bianchi says, shaking his head with a smile.

"You told him?" Maria asks, having appeared seemingly out of nowhere, flushed and sweaty from the field. Pierre and Del Orbe follow closely behind her, still unable to keep up. Our seventh period is over, and it's finally time for dinner.

"Told him what?" Pierre asks.

"Rambeau and Danvers are taking flying lessons. That's where they've been going," Bianchi says.

"I told you guys," Del Orbe says.

"No, you didn't. You said that they were going to the airport to *watch* planes, not to *fly* planes," Pierre says.

"Were you at the airport?" Del Orbe asks us, building his case.

"Yes, but—"

"Were you watching planes?" Del Orbe is now pacing in front of us as if we're on the stand.

"Yes," Maria says.

"Overruled!" Del Orbe says, pounding his hand into the air in front of Pierre.

"What are you even doing?" Bianchi asks, laughing.

"Not guilty, Your Honor! I win the bet," Del Orbe says, striding toward Mitchell Hall, his arm raised high in victory.

"And you wonder why we didn't tell you sooner," I say. We follow behind Del Orbe.

"Oh, I didn't wonder why you never told us," Bianchi says.

"You owe me a soda," Del Orbe yells over his shoulder.

"We don't owe you nothing," Pierre mumbles, running to catch up.

"Did he ever tell you why he named the plane *Mr. Goodnight*?" Bianchi asks.

I shake my head. "He said he would after we flew him, but he never did."

"I mean, it's nothing good, right? You don't name

a plane *Mr. Goodnight* because things were going well," Bianchi says.

"I think things always went well for *Mr. Goodnight*," I say.

"Just not anyone else," Maria says, laughing.

As we walk into dinner, I'm uneasy at how much I need my and Maria's plan to work. I'm haunted by the vastness of my now-realized dream of flying and the fear that resounding, life-changing *click* could easily be taken from me if all these pieces don't fall into place.

I know that's not how it works. Even if we don't get to where we want to be, the experience won't have been for nothing. The knowing, though, seems to be stuck at the topmost layer of my brain, along with what year the Gettysburg Address was given and the different parts of an atom.

I know it academically. Intellectually. Logically.

Just like Jack said: Even if you're the best pilot in the world, sometimes things go wrong.

But how am I supposed to come to terms with this? How am I supposed to be okay with not being allowed to do something I was born to do, not because I'm not good enough or because I didn't earn it, but simply because I'm a woman?

I'm *never* going to be okay with that.

"Attention!" Maria says, calling our group to order as Captain Jenks approaches. All of us face him and salute. We remain at attention as Jenks looks us over, covered in sweat and grass stains. Bianchi and I are at the end of the line because we were lagging behind the group on our way to Mitchell. I'm hoping this one time Jenks won't single me out and humiliate me. I look straight ahead, feeling Bianchi, solid and unmoving, next to me. I swear I can feel the atmospheric pressure around our group change as Jenks comes to a stop in front of me. I stand firm, unblinking. Shoulders pushed back. Chin up. Back strong.

"Airman Danvers, I'm thrilled you'll be joining us at the air show tomorrow," Jenks says.

"Yes, sir," I say, my voice clipped and efficient.

"I've given much thought to Cadet Instructor Pilot Wolff's words regarding the ability of . . . well, *certain people*, to be taught, and I believe you will find tomorrow's excursion highly educational," Jenks says.

"Yes, sir," I say, his words bringing me underwater.

"I'd like you to be especially mindful as you take stock of the pilots. I'm curious, Airman Danvers, if you will be able to see the difference between them and you."

"Yes, sir," I say, drowning.

"You do want to prove Cadet Instructor Pilot Wolff

right, don't you?" Jenks leans in, voice lowered. "That you can be taught?" His voice is muffled and far away. As close as I've become to my friends, I've never felt more alone.

"Yes, sir." I am shutting down. Disappearing.

"So, let us see if tomorrow is when you finally learn just exactly how fundamentally you do not fit in amongst the ranks of those esteemed pilots. A cursory glance should be all it takes"—Jenks circles behind me—"to illuminate your shortcomings."

BLACK.

"Yes, sir." My own voice is elsewhere. Outside of myself.

As our interaction ends, the group salutes Jenks, and without another word, he continues on with a contented sigh. It's Maria I see first. Appearing in front of me, as if from nowhere.

"—okay? Danvers? Are you okay?" Her face is blurry and her voice is somewhere far off. Bianchi's hand is tight around my upper arm, and it takes me a few seconds to realize that he is, in fact, holding me up. Del Orbe and Pierre pace and loom behind, worried and frustrated that they're unable to help.

"Why does he hate me?" I ask. I can feel the sadness and the rage and the defeat and the pain and the hopelessness and the confusion sitting on my chest, ripping at the sides of my throat as they claw their way up.

"Because you're the best," Del Orbe says. I can hear the frustration in his voice. We all turn around. He's shaking his head and pacing.

"But doesn't he want us to be the best?" I ask, hating how much Jenks continues to get to me.

"Yeah, he'll let us be great as long as we act exactly like him," Pierre says bitterly.

"Jenks was a Thunderbird. He flew combat. He was the you of his class. So how is he supposed to still experience the pride that comes with being a member of a super-exclusive club if he feels like they're just starting to let anyone in?" Maria reasons.

"In some sick way, I bet he believes he's protecting the sanctity of his post," Bianchi says.

"And that's when they start saying things like . . ." Del Orbe thinks. " 'You've got such natural talent.' "

" 'You're lucky,' " Maria says.

" 'You're too much of a showoff,' " Pierre says.

"See, you forgot to ask permission, Danvers," Del Orbe says.

"You forgot to be grateful," Maria says.

As they stand around me, I don't know what to say.

No, that's not quite right. I don't want to say anything. I want to scream. Roar. Run over to Jenks, pin him down, and make him listen to me as I outline all the ways that he's wrong.

He is wrong.

Right?

CHAPTER 12

"I GOT EVERYONE THE SAME THING. I COULDN'T remember—just, take 'em," Bianchi says, handing us each a soda.

"You panicked," I say, taking Pierre's and mine from him.

"I did not panic. I made an executive decision," Bianchi says, passing the last two sodas down to Maria and Del Orbe.

"He panicked," Del Orbe seconds, right before everyone else echoes him.

"You're welcome, strangers who used to be my friends," Bianchi says, sitting down next to me.

"Ladies and gentlemen!" The voice booms through the loudspeaker and all five of us immediately sit up straight and look to the skies. "We want to welcome you to today's air show!"

A B-52 bomber streaks across the sky, its high-pitched scream of an engine forcing some in the audience to cover their ears as it roars overhead. The bomber's almost birdlike cry belies the plane's absolute gigantic wingspan. All of us lean into the sound.

"Okay, that was cool." Maria sounds like she's a kid again. I look over at her beaming face, finally beginning to let go of the lingering stench of yesterday's run-in with Jenks.

The announcer comes back on and introduces a helicopter aerobatics team out of Houston.

"I saw the Silver Eagles back when I was a kid. They're disbanded now but, man, they were cool," Pierre shouts over the rumble and din of the air show.

"What a shock! Pierre talking about helicopters," Del Orbe says. We watch as the helicopters zoom and whip around, smoke spilling from behind them. By their fourth trick, what we're watching doesn't even feel real.

"They made me want to fly. Made me want to join up," Pierre says.

"Please tell me you're aware you've told us this literally a thousand times," Bianchi says to Pierre.

"Which is a mere sliver of the times you've talked

about wanting to fly combat, so . . ." Pierre trails off. Bianchi feigns as if he's been truly shattered.

"Not to change the subject, but—" Del Orbe cuts in.

"Totally doing it anyway," Maria finishes.

Del Orbe barks out a laugh and continues. "I want to make sure we get over to see Senator John Glenn. He's got a meet-and-greet over by the stage. I've got a list of questions, and I plan on following each and every piece of advice he gives me to a tee," he says.

"What a shock! Del Orbe talking about becoming an astronaut," Pierre says. Del Orbe shoves Pierre and they dissolve into laughter.

"We're going. And that's that," Del Orbe says.

"No. No way. I'd just make a fool of myself," Bianchi says, his face flushing.

"Oh, you should go talk to him. I mean, why not, right?" I ask, nudging him.

"Why not? Did you not hear when I said that I would just make a fool out of myself?" he asks.

I clap my hands together. "It's decided. We're going. When is it?" I ask Maria.

"Three p.m.," Maria says.

"Done," I say. And everyone just moves on as Bianchi seems to slowly descend into panic about the upcoming event.

The helicopters finish up and the unmistakable growl and purr of an engine begins rumbling closer and closer to the show center.

"No," I say in disbelief. "No way. It can't be."

"Why wouldn't they mention it?" Maria asks.

"What are you two talking about?" Bianchi asks.

The 1942 Stearman PT-17 roars across the sky, and Maria and I hoot and holler as the announcer introduces Jack and Bonnie.

"Gentlemen, meet *Mr. Goodnight*," Maria says, jerking her thumb toward the sky.

"Are you kidding me?" Bianchi asks. *Mr. Goodnight* climbs into the horizon, rolling and dropping like a leaf once it reaches its maximum altitude.

"How is that the same plane we fly every Sunday?" Maria asks, watching as it moves through the scattered clouds like it's a metal toy in a child's hand, impossibly curving and dipping across the field in ways that seem to defy physics or logic. The plane climbs again, banking left and then falling into a spiral, looking like it's lost power. Maria and I lean forward, not knowing whether or not the plane is actually dropping from above, and suddenly fearful for the pilots we know are within its clutches. I grab Maria's hand, terrified that I'm about to watch—

And then *Mr. Goodnight* roars to life and the crowd goes wild.

"Good night," I say, finally exhaling. Maria and I look at one another.

"Is that . . . ? Do you . . . ? That can't be why they named him that, can it?" Maria asks.

"That's definitely not why they named him that," Bianchi says, watching as the plane rolls across the sky once more. The crowd is on their feet applauding the performance, and we join them.

We see an F-14 Tomcat demonstration and watch in amazement as a tiny woman walks on the wings of on old-timey biplane. There are parachute teams and even a 1929 Tri-Motor plane that looks sleek and modern in all its silver-and-blue glory. There's even a sky-diving clown at one point.

And then.

"Ladies and gentlemen. Your United States Air Force Thunderbirds are extremely pleased to be with you here today." The crowd gets to their feet once more. This is what we all came for. The announcer continues, "If you look to the show center, you'll see the Thunderbird maintenance crews and Thunderbird pilots beginning their march out to their aircraft." All eyes turn to the columns of men walking toward the six beautiful F-16 planes on the other side of the airfield.

"Those F-Sixteens," Maria breathes out as she trails off.

Six F-16 Fighting Falcons sit in the middle of the airfield. Painted white with red and blue accents, they're the most beautiful things I've ever seen.

"By the end of the day, I'm going to touch one of those planes," I announce.

"I know what you mean? But, that sounded super weird," Maria says, laughing.

"You should have seen the hand gesture I held back for your sake," I say.

"Let's see it, Danvers," she says. I reach out the palm of my hand and reverently close my eyes as if I'm feeling the warm heat from a crackling fire. I pop open my eyes, pull back my arm, and can't keep from laughing.

We turn our attention back to the field as one by one, the Thunderbirds climb into their planes. It is not lost on any of us that every single Thunderbird looks exactly like Jenks.

I can actually feel the heaviness settle around all five of us as Jenks's words return to each one of us and remind us who we are, and more importantly, who we aren't.

"Fig Newton," Pierre blurts.

"What?" Maria asks.

"Lloyd 'Fig' Newton. I can't believe I forgot," Pierre says. On the airfield the Thunderbirds begin their ground checks.

"What are you talking about?" Del Orbe asks.

"An African American flyer who was a Thunderbird back in the seventies, and—just to be clear, because I know we're all thinking it—no, he looked nothing like Jenks," Pierre says. All five of us look out to the airfield. "If he can do it . . ."

"So can we," I finish. Pierre looks over and nods.

"So can we," he repeats.

The F-16s boom to life.

"And now, ladies and gentlemen, let's begin today's flying demonstration!"

Four of the F-16s roar across the sky in an arrowhead formation.

"Look at that," Del Orbe calls out, pointing to the underside of the planes, where a giant blue Native American–style Thunderbird is painted.

"Why only four?" I ask.

"The other two are solos," Pierre says.

The F-16s go from an arrowhead formation into arrowhead rolls. The planes are so close together it's like someone has hung them on a wall using a level and ruler. They're so perfectly measured that it's easy to forget that each one is probably going about a thousand miles per hour at any given time.

The two solo pilots do opposing four-point rolls right at the show center. From the left, the other four planes zoom toward us in a diamond formation. The arrangement transitions seamlessly into a diamond roll, and before our goose pimples have dissipated from the last trick, we're told to look out onto the horizon for the two solo planes approaching getting ready to do a crossover break—which just looks like the scariest game of chicken in the entire world.

I can't catch my breath when the two solo planes scream past each other, and next our attention is directed toward the other four planes, who are now approaching in a trail formation. We're told that Thunderbird One (the leader) will call for a change back into the diamond formation. It's like we're watching the intricate dials and cogs inside a clock as the wingman and slot pilot move into their diamond positions.

Then, out of nowhere, one of the solo planes is looping around in the far horizon. His job, the announcer tells us, is to catch up to the diamond formation. The plane is now going upwards of ten miles a minute and his task is to catch the other four planes right in front of the crowd. The entire audience is quiet. The solo plane screams past the diamond formation right at the show center, and the crowd goes wild. He overtakes the formation, who then climb high into the sky wingtip to wingtip.

"This is the move they're known for," Maria says, barely able to contain herself.

"The Bomb Burst and Crossover," Pierre says, to no one and everyone. All five of us are rapt as the diamond formation does a rolling climb higher and higher and higher. Each plane drops away, falling like a leaf on the wind, white smoke billowing from behind them. The Bomb Burst fills up the entire sky as the four planes leave a pocket of smoke exactly at the show center.

"If they do the Crossover again . . . all the smoke . . ." I worry.

"They've got this," Maria says.

The smoke from the Bomb Burst fills the sky, and we can only sit by and watch as the two solo planes begin their approach for yet another Crossover. But this time they will be doing their trick in a sky completely filled with smoke. They won't be able to see one another. I watch one plane, then the other, then back to the first. I have no idea how close they are to each other.

"They're going to collide!" I say, and Maria takes my hand and holds it tight.

At a thousand miles per hour it takes mere seconds for the two planes to speed past each other with what looks like no space at all between them, only a hair-breadth apart.

"See?" Maria says. I look from her down to my hand, where her fingers left a clear indentation. "Never doubted it for a second."

"Uh-huh," I say, rolling my eyes and massaging my knuckles.

"That was incredible!" Pierre says.

The announcer thanks the Thunderbirds and reminds us that John Glenn will be making his appearance later on this afternoon, then hypes us all up for a performance by a funk band that'll be closing out the air show.

"John Glenn, THEN a funk band? What kind of dream day is this?" Bianchi says as we are herded out of the bleachers along with the thousands of other spectators.

"I'm still going to touch one of those planes," I say, noticing that the Thunderbirds have not only climbed down from their F-16s, but now they're walking out into the crowds and shaking hands and signing pictures. I scan the crowds behind them and notice they're allow-ing people to walk back and look at the F-16s.

This is my shot. I look over at Maria. She's thinking the same thing.

"We're going to go stand in line to meet Senator Glenn, so we'll meet you over there after you . . . touch a plane," Bianchi says skeptically, trying to humor me but looking at me like I'm a crazy person.

"Maria wants to touch the plane too now," I say. All eyes turn to Maria.

"Fine. I, too, am a plane-toucher," Maria says.

"Plane-toucher," Pierre says, and he can't keep from giggling.

"You go touch your plane, then, ladies, and I'll meet an American hero," Del Orbe says.

"Oh no, wait a minute. We're meeting Senator Glenn. Just—"

"After you touch a plane, we know," Bianchi says with a laugh, waving good-bye as we go our separate ways.

Maria and I snake through the crowd toward the airfield. We can barely contain ourselves. Today has been magical. Truly magical. A reminder about what all this is about: not Jenks. Not trying to prove myself. Not any of that.

It's about the love of flying.

Period.

I smile and, oh man, it feels so good. Maria and I pick up our pace, and by the end of our trek, we're almost running in anticipation.

The crowd around the Thunderbirds has lessened somewhat, so it doesn't take us very long to get to the head of the group. There, at the front of our sector, is one of the Thunderbirds. He's tall, imposing, and just like Jenks said, he looks nothing like me. Maria and I finally reach him.

"Well, hey there," he says, signing a picture of the planes in one of their formations.

"We're fourth-class cadets, sir," I say, trying not to pick apart how young I sound.

"Your families must be so proud of you," he says, handing us each a photo.

"They are, sir," Maria says.

"I wish my daughter was here to meet you two," he says, taking off his sunglasses. His hooded brown eyes are . . . kind. Maybe he doesn't look like Jenks as much as I thought when I'd first seen the Thunderbirds striding across the field.

"Sir?" I ask.

"She's still little, but she's always dreamed of flying."

It sounds like he's about to say more, but just then he's mobbed by an entire classroom of hopped-up kindergartners. Maria and I stand there for a second, not sure if we heard him right.

"Did he say what I think he said?" I ask.

"He did," Maria says solemnly. We stand there for a few seconds in a daze.

"We've got a plane to touch," I finally say, beelining for the one F-16 they've offered up to the air show spectators. Maria and I circle the plane in a sort of haze of admiration and respect. We lose sight of each other, both in our own worlds.

Up close the plane is exquisite. Sleek and powerful. Elegant and deceptively simple. I crane my neck, and my eyes fixate on the cockpit.

I step forward and right there, right below the cockpit, I reach out my hand and lay it on the body of the plane. The metal is smooth, and the feel of it beneath my hand pulls me in.

"Someday," I say to the plane, my hand lingering.

CHAPTER 13

"YOU'RE PULLING UP TOO EARLY, DANVERS. DO it again. Let's see if the sixth time is the charm," Jack says through the radio.

I groan audibly. Today is our final flying lesson, and true to what he promised back when we took our first hop together, Jack is insisting that we spend it teaching me how to crash. Or as he likes to call it, *power-off stall*. Maria, by the way, spent her last hop doing a series of slow barrel rolls, just like Bonnie had promised. Not that I'm bitter or anything.

The first time we try this fun little power-off stall, I nervously (and quite rightfully) blow the horn twice because we are in fact, crashing. I wait for Jack to do something. Jump to my aid? Save the day? Instead, all I hear crackling through the radio is his dry, smoky voice utter one word: "Nope." I level the plane out and he just tells me to do it again.

"Let's start over. Reduce the throttle," Jack says, and I follow his instructions to the letter. I can't stop my hands from shaking. *Deep breath. Okay . . . focus.* I blink my eyes and try to pull my shoulders back. Another deep breath, trying to steady myself. "Let the nose fall. Let it fall, Danvers. To the horizon, not below it. Let him drop. Reduce the power to idle. All the way, Danvers. Keep pulling the stick back. What happens if these movements aren't coordinated?"

"I'd go into a spin," I yell, more for myself than Jack, as I know he can't hear me, and I also know he knows I'm terrifyingly aware that the consequence for doing this wrong is spinning out or just flat-out falling from the sky. No pressure, though.

"Hold the nose, Danvers. Hold the nose—" And that's when the stall horn starts blaring. One might argue that this blaring siren is telling me to stop what I'm doing and try to fix things. That even *Mr. Goodnight* thinks this is a bad idea. But apparently not. We're to the point where I've pulled up *Mr. Goodnight* on my last five attempts. One millisecond after that stall horn sounds and I'm taking the plane back to full power. But not this time.

Hold the nose, Danvers. At the horizon, not below it. Hold the nose. The plane is losing power. Mr. Goodnight *is going night-night. We're falling. We're falling. And then the plane just . . . stops.*

We are crashing.

The nose of the plane dips. It's too quiet, save for the blaring stall horn and the muffled screams inside my own head.

"Wait for the break, Danvers," comes the voice over the radio. "Wait for it."

Every sensation in my body is telling me to pull this plane up. To save myself. To fix this. To be right. *Fight it, Danvers. Fight it. I can do this. Wait for the break. Trust myself. Come on. I got this.* My hand grips the throttle. My breathing steadies. My eyes focus.

Feel it. Wait . . . wait . . . hold it . . . just—

There. THERE! The break. I can feel it. I CAN FEEL IT.

And I give *Mr. Goodnight* full power, pull the nose back to the horizon, right the rudder, bring the flaps up, and recover the plane to cruise altitude.

"Now, there you go, Danvers! There you go!" Jack says through the radio, his voice radiating pride. It's the first time he's ever sounded this excited about something other than his wife's cherry pie.

"I DID IT! Woo-hoo!" I grab the air horn and honk it and honk it and honk it and honk it. Apparently four honks means *I conquered my fears and trusted myself.*

"Now, let's do it again," Jack says.

And I can't wait to try.

After I do another three power-off stalls—and I officially pass the forty-hour threshold required to take my private pilot's license exam, Jack's voice breaks through the radio.

"Take this plane home and land it," Jack says. My heart soars.

This is the first time Jack has let me land *Mr. Goodnight* all on my own.

I can barely contain myself. I sweep *Mr. Goodnight* around and head back to hangar thirty-nine.

"Land on your own terms, Danvers. Not theirs," Jack counsels as I descend from the clouds. He spends the whole time talking to me, directing, guiding. About having to splash the plane and putting *Mr. Goodnight* in the drink if need be. Talking to the tower, checking the sky, lining the plane up with the runway, keeping my head, less power and more power, and then the ground speeds closer and closer, and I've never felt more alive than when I feel all three of *Mr. Goodnight*'s tires hit the runway . . . with maybe only a couple* of bounces.

"Wooo-hooooo!" I yell, thrusting a fist into the air.

"No bounce would have been better, Danvers, but nicely done," Jack says as we slow down and taxi off the runway and over to hangar thirty-nine.

I hop down from *Mr. Goodnight* and wait as Jack navigates his way down from the rear cockpit.

"How do you feel?" he asks as we walk back to the hangar.

"Super ready for the test. Maria and I made flash cards, and we've been studying every night. We know we're going to nail the written and the practical; it's the oral that's—"

"Danvers." Jack stops me.

"You okay? Everything okay?" I ask. "What? Did I . . . Did I do something wrong?"

"No, kiddo," he says.

"Then what is it?"

"Are you proud of yourself, Carol?" He asks.

"What?" His question has taken me completely off guard.

---

* more than a couple

"Are you. Proud of. Yourself?" he asks again, cutting the simple sentence into even smaller chunks so I can follow.

My mind is a riot of different excuses and ways to water down my emotions, the impulse to say that sure, I'm proud but Jack is such a good teacher and maybe it was easy and I still haven't passed the test yet and I still haven't made the Flying Falcons yet and is there anything really to be proud of if all this was for nothing?

Jack waits. I look away from him. Cross and uncross and recross my arms over my chest. Sigh. Shake my head. Fighting it. Just like I fought pulling up *Mr. Goodnight* until I felt the break.

Feel the break, Danvers.

It starts with a warmth in my middle. Scary and intensifying. I feel like laughing and crying at the same time. I breathe through it. *Don't fight. Trust myself. I can do this.* I finally allow that warmth to swell and radiate throughout my whole body. And when I look back up at Jack, my eyes are welling with tears.

"Yes, sir. I am so proud of myself," I say, my voice choked and hoarse. He smiles that crooked smile of his, gives me an efficient nod, and continues toward the hangar. But, just as he passes me, he stops.

"You're a good pilot, Danvers," Jack says. I nod,

acknowledging that I heard and won't try to talk him out of it this time.

"Thank you, sir," I say. A quick wink and Jack disappears into the hangar.

Maria and I are still buzzing as we drive back to campus later that afternoon.

"The first time we tried the slow roll, I pulled through and didn't go right into the roll. I just froze right there, right when I was upside down, of course. The whole world was . . . down there, and I was here, and I was positive that my belts were going to give way." Maria is talking a million miles an hour and using her hands so emphatically that she hits one on the passenger's-side window at one point. She absently massages her knuckle where it made contact. "Bonnie jumped in and had to finish the roll. Did you know her family were farmers and that she flew their crop duster? That's how she got started. And she would just . . . start rolling the plane FOR FUN. No one even taught her. Can you imagine? Being like fifteen and just . . . rolling a plane over?" Maria sits back in her seat, takes a deep breath, shoots her arms straight forward, and whoops. "That was the coolest!" I look over, and Maria has tucked all our paperwork tight under her leg. Jack and Bonnie gave us everything we needed so we can go in next Sunday and take our test.

I hum along in agreement, but now that the sheer elation of the moment has begun to wear off, I'm overcome by a feeling beyond pure excitement. The truth is, I get more nervous every step we take closer to our goal.

I almost crashed a plane today. But what scared me far more was allowing that feeling of pride to finally spread through me untethered.

I am a good pilot.

Why is that so hard for me to own? It's not bragging, it's just accurate.

"You're such a good pilot, Maria," I say, as we finally pull into the campus.

"What?" She looks like I just slapped her. I park the Mustang and we climb out.

"You're a good pilot. That slow roll was . . . It was beautiful. And that was just the brilliant thing you did *today*," I say. Maria smiles and looks away from me. I watch as she fights the compliment. Just as I did.

"Thank you." It's two simple words that come at last, but it took an internal war in order for her to say them.

The cold settles around us as we hurry through

campus back to our dorm room, and I wonder why I don't feel as good as I should, knowing how far I've come this year. I know I'm stubborn. I know that my drive can be a bit laser-focused. I've known for some time that I see showing vulnerability in any way as a weakness. I've known that my need to be right often supersedes my need to be happy. And I know, more than anything else in the world, that in order for me to feel any kind of pride in myself I needed it cosigned by someone really important,* like I acknowledged earlier in the situation with Jenks.

So why don't I feel better now that I've faced these issues through every day spent on this campus, through every session with Jack and Bonnie? Instead, I just feel like I've missed something. And that the other shoe is about to drop, taking with it all of my best-laid plans.

"You okay?" Maria asks as we get ready for bed later that night. "You've been kinda quiet."

"I think I'm just nervous," I say, crawling under my covers. Maria closes her journal, turns out the light, and gets into her bed.

"Nervous about what?" Her voice fills the dark room.

---

*not me

"Everything," I say, before I can stop myself.

"Me too," she says. I whip over onto my side.

"Really?"

"Uh, yeah. This whole plan thing was, I don't know, kind of far off for a long time, and now that it's here and . . ." Maria trails off.

"You realize how much you want it," I finish.

"That and . . . I realize how much maybe I don't deserve it," Maria says.

"I so get that," I say, flipping onto my back and staring up at the dark ceiling.

"And I hate it, right? It's not fair," she continues. "If my accomplishments were a scientific study or some math problem I'd have to solve, it'd be super obvious that whoever did this stuff equals someone who deserves to be in those top slots. But, it's like I add up all the numbers, study all the data, come up with my conclusions, and then at the bottom of the column I see my name, and then somehow it erases all the data and the facts and the proof and just leaves this giant shrug of an answer. Like, because it's me, it doesn't count, for some reason."

"Being the best was much easier when I thought it was just about coming in first," I say.

"Right? Who could argue that?"

"But now—I don't know—it feels like way more than that." I remember my conversation with Bianchi at Acceptance. "I thought integrity was just about how I treated other people."

"No, I know. We have to have it for ourselves, too."

"Ugh, it sounds so cheesy, though."

"Right? I wanted to find a way that I didn't sound like some after-school special."

I hear Maria shift in her bed, and when she next speaks, her voice is dripping with saccharine and has taken on a strange accent. "You've got to love yourself before anyone else will, dear!"

"How do you not roll your eyes at that?" I ask, laughing.

We are quiet.

"I am a good pilot." Maria's voice resonates through the room. Strong and proud. A wide smile breaks across my face. I know how hard that was for her to say, because I had to say it too, in one way or another, to Jack earlier today.

"I am a good pilot," I echo.

It's quiet for a long time. Until . . .

"We're so cheesy," Maria says, and I can feel her smile in the darkness.

"So cheesy," I repeat, laughing.

CHAPTER 14

MARIA AND I TAKE OUR PRIVATE PILOT'S LICENSE tests.

When we asked how long it'd take to get our results, the woman shrugged her shoulders and estimated a month or two. If it takes one month, everything is fine. If it takes two, all this was for nothing.* Cue: one air horn honk.

So, we wait.

And life kind of goes back to normal, whatever that is.

Study sessions in McDermott, yelling *That's Flickerball*

---

*Ugh, fine. Except building character, becoming an overall better person, and realizing I don't have to constantly prove myself.

at Pierre whenever we get the chance, and trying to stay out of Jenks's way. I'd been fully expecting him to come back over to me at the next Soaring class and ask if I'd learned anything at the air show like he'd asked.

I had my answer—more of a speech, really—all planned. It was going to be this masterwork of a monologue that used his direct quotes—which I can recall verbatim, since they're burned into my memory—as jumping-off points to disprove everything he said. It starts out, *I took more than a cursory glance, sir* . . . then wends its way around talk about relics, the future, and evolution. I even practiced where in the speech to look him straight in the eye and where to pause for effect. I was kind of hoping he'd approach me at the air show so I could take a moment to dramatically look from him to the actual Thunderbirds as I talked about how it was he who no longer belonged, not us. Which is when he would burst into tears and admit how blind he's been, and then I'm both right and happy (because there's no logical reason those two things can't coexist) as the rest of the Soaring class, led by Wolff, lifts me on their shoulders right after thanking me for finally taking Jenks down a peg.

But Jenks hasn't so much as looked my way for the last several weeks. And the sick part is . . . I kind of miss it. What I didn't tell anyone, not even Maria, is that I want Jenks to either hate me or admire me. I don't know what to do with indifference.

"You heading over?" Bianchi asks, catching up to me on my way over to Soaring.

"Yeah," I say noticing he's holding a notebook in his hand. Not one that I recognize. "What's that?"

"I found it in my last class. It's Noble's. Was wondering if you'd give it to her later at the dorm," he says, handing me the notebook.

"Oh, sure," I say, taking it.

"I had to kind of page through it to find out whose it was, though, and—" I look over at him. "I swear it wasn't snooping. I was honestly just looking for a name."

"Yes, I have met you before, Bianchi." He looks over at me. "You're talking to me like I don't know that you'd never snoop in someone's stuff." I shrug. "You wouldn't."

"Oh. Well . . . right," he says, nodding firmly.

"So you found Noble's notebook and . . . ?"

"Did you know she wants to be an astronaut?" he asks.

"What? No way," I say, not really thinking Noble wanted to be anything except chronically annoyed.

"I know. I thought Del Orbe was the only person we

knew who was planning on going to NASA after this," Bianchi says.

I nod. "Right?"

"They'd be lucky to have them both," Bianchi says. He looks over and quite rightly is a bit thrown that I'm now looking up at him with a goofy smile on my face.

"What?" He swipes at the corners of his mouth. "Do I have toothpaste, or . . . ?" He swipes at his nose.

"No, and also it's two thirty in the afternoon. Why would you have toothpaste on your face?"

"Let's just move on," Bianchi says, taking one last pass at his face.

"I was just going to say that I was wrong about you," I say. Bianchi looks down at me, shocked.

"What?" he asks incredulously. "Did I just hear Carol Danvers admit she was wrong? That alone is worthy of a Thunderbird flyover."

I bark out a laugh. "Carol Danvers can also take back the nice thing she just said if you'd like."

"No, it's—" Bianchi smiles, almost to himself. "Thanks—it . . . I don't know, it means a lot."

I smile back. "You're welcome." Bianchi and I arrive at class just as everyone is gathering.

"So you'll get Noble her notebook?" he says to me.

"Yep."

"There's just a lot of personal stuff in there. I wouldn't want . . . I just don't want it to get in the wrong hands, you know?" I nod as Bianchi peels off toward the far side of the field, where his group is set up for Soaring, throwing me one last backward glance. I hold up Noble's notebook and give it a little wave, signaling that I will remember and will get it to her.

"Airman Danvers." Jenks. I stop. Stand at attention. Salute. "What items is a fourth-class cadet supposed to have when attending Introduction to Soaring?" I quickly and efficiently rattle off the items we are supposed to have with us during class.

"So you know the rules, yet you insist upon not following them," he says as he paces in front of me.

"Sir?" I ask, not sure what I've done wrong.

"The notebook," Jenks says. I see out of the corner of my eye Noble walk past, clock me and Jenks in a situation that looks like it's about to be me getting in trouble, and then the horror on her face as she sees the notebook in my hand that she recognizes as her own. A notebook filled with such private things that Tom Bianchi made sure to hand-deliver it to someone who could get it to her as discreetly as possible.

"Yes, sir," I say, keeping my voice as neutral as possible.

"Is this your notebook, Airman Danvers?" Jenks asks. I feel Noble's gaze on me, her entire face reddening, even as I keep my eyes forward and my features impassive.

"Yes, sir," I say. Out of the corner of my eye I see Noble's entire body deflate, the relief washing over her. Jenks begins to circle me, his hands clasped behind his back, thumb twitching. I brace myself.

"Several weeks ago I tasked you with something." I can see Maria and Pierre in the distance.

"Yes, sir."

"What was it I asked you to do?"

"To take a cursory glance at the esteemed pilots at the air show and finally learn just exactly how fundamentally I don't fit in," I say, repeating his words verbatim, just as I'd practiced. But somehow I don't think the rest of my speech is about to go as planned.

"And is Cadet Instructor Wolff correct? That despite your inability to follow simple orders you can actually be taught?" I see Wolff strapping in one of the other airmen for their fourth and final hop in the glider. I was all set to go up third. Today was supposed to be awesome.

"Yes, sir."

"And what did you learn?" The notebook is heavy in my hand.

"You were right, sir," I say.

The slightest of smiles ghosts across Jenks's face. "I must say I am pleasantly surprised. Please, do go on."

"That after a cursory glance it does appear that I do not, in fact, fit in with those esteemed pilots, but—"

"But?" Jenks's lip curls.

"I took more than a cursory glance, sir."

"Did you?"

"Yes, sir."

"And tell me, Airman Danvers. What did you find?"

"That you are a relic, Captain Jenks. And it is you who does not belong among those esteemed pilots." I make eye contact with him. "Not me."

Not the speech, exactly. But something . . .

I wait. I wait for the tears and the hoisting onto shoulders. I wait for the thrill of being right to firework all over my body. Instead—

"Relic, derived from the Latin word *reliquiae*, meaning *remains*. I am remains? Perhaps it is the thirteenth-century definition you are referencing used to describe the remains of a holy person or a martyr. While I do think quite highly of myself, I do not imagine myself to be a holy person nor a martyr. Do you?" Jenks begins to circle me, hands clasped lazily behind his back. "Sadly, Airman Danvers, your low intelligence has led you to choose the wrong word and, once again, humiliate yourself." Jenks begins to walk away. "Shame, really. Feels like you actually practiced that speech."

And everything goes . . . RED.

"Maria and I are going to try out for the Flying Falcons!" I yell after him, unable to stop myself. Captain Jenks doesn't even deign to turn around.

"Unless you have somehow managed to get your private pilot's licenses since last we spoke, Danvers—"

"We got them," I lie, the words tumbling out.

Jenks turns around, his lips curling into the faintest of smiles. And in that instant, I hear *Mr. Goodnight*'s blaring stall horn. And I know that I've pulled up too early. I didn't trust myself to feel the break. Again. I needed to be right. More important, I needed to prove *him* wrong.

"So you and Airman Rambeau think you'll be trying out for the Flying Falcons after all." I flick my gaze over to where Maria is now watching, unmoving—her life in my hands as the plane spins out toward the ground. What have I done?

"Yes, sir," I say, trying to calm down and wishing I could take it all back.

"Well, then let's see if this old relic can do anything to keep that from happening," Jenks says. He looks from me over to Maria, and I see his disdainful gaze hit her like a truck. Then he shakes his head, turns, and walks on.

Soaring class is a blur. I can't focus. I need to talk to Maria. Make it right. Do something. Take it back. Fix this.

As class ends, I run over to her.

"I'm so sorry," I say, catching up to her. She looks over at me. Her face is creased in hurt and confusion.

"Why? Why'd you do it?" she asks. Her voice is a wounded plea, and I almost wish she was furious instead. Facing her anger would be easier than facing her sadness. It breaks my heart.

"I don't know—I . . . Captain Jenks—"

"Captain Jenks. I am so sick of hearing about Captain Jenks. You keep knocking on that door and all you're going to get is bloody knuckles. He is never going to open that door and welcome you in. Ever." Maria steps closer to me. "You need to decide how long, and just what you're willing to sacrifice, in order to keep believing that his way is the only way."

I've thought this countless times, but hearing some-one else make this observation about me just emphasizes how lousy I feel about letting this happen, that despite how far I've come, here I am, falling prey to old ways once again. "Maria, please."

Maria takes my hands and squeezes so tight. "I love you, Danvers. I really do. But you need to figure this one out on your own." Maria runs to catch up to Bianchi and Pierre, who have been waiting respect-fully just outside of earshot, leaving me wretchedly and rightfully alone.

"I love you, too," I say to no one.

"Yeah, okay," Noble says, appearing as if from nowhere.

"It's . . ." I meekly point in Maria's direction, but then . . . "Never mind."

"I believe you have something of mine," she says, looking down at the notebook clasped in my hand.

"Oh, yeah." I hand the notebook to her.

"You didn't have to do that, you know," she says, unable to meet my eyes.

"Yeah, I did." I watch as Maria, Bianchi, and Pierre turn the corner and disappear into campus. Noble flicks through the notebook, scanning its contents, making sure everything is just as she left it.

"I saw my whole life pass before my eyes when I thought Jenks was going to get his hands on it," Noble says, stopping at one point in the notebook. Her gaze softens and her fingers gently fix and shift something folded and hidden in its lined pages. "It's so stupid. I don't even know why I keep it." She looks up, and with a decisive sigh, hands me the folded-up piece of paper.

"You have a right to know what you were protecting," she says.

I take the paper. It feels like tissue, so delicate and hopelessly fragile. I carefully unfold it to find a child's colorful drawing of a little girl with flaming-red hair dressed up as an astronaut, floating among the stars. I stare at the drawing, my eyes welling with tears. The little girl's stick arms, the zigzagging circle of a body, the wobbly red smile that traces the width of her giant head.

"It's wonderful," I choke out.

This is what I've forgotten. This is who I've forgotten.

My entire childhood was spent drawing pictures of me and planes. In planes. Next to planes. As a plane. Walls and refrigerators overrun with them. Stacks and stacks. Stick-figure arms wide, wobbly smile taking up my whole giant potato-shaped head. Soaring in the Crayola-blue sky along with round, puffy clouds and a banana-yellow sun that wore giant, oversize sunglasses.

I hand Noble back her drawing. She carefully folds up the paper and places it delicately back in the middle of the notebook. She closes the cover and pulls the book up to her chest, her arms tightly crossing over it.

"You going to be okay?" Noble asks.

Such a simple question.

I'm tempted to throw back some completely adequate answer about being fine. Be glib, be cool. Shrug off all that I've learned about myself since coming here until after I find out if I passed my private pilot's license test and after I try out for the Flying Falcons and after I get everything I've ever wanted.

But none of that matters if this is who I have to become in order to achieve it.

My mind flashes back to Noble's treasured drawing. Back to my own childhood bedroom completely wallpapered in drawings of a future where the only thing I wanted to do was fly.

No Jenks. No proving myself. No knocking on some door that's never going to open. I remember the wobbly smile taking up the most space on the page.

Joy.

"I'm working on it," I say.

CHAPTER 15

WHEN I GET TO OUR USUAL TABLE IN THE MESS
hall, there's a full-blown argument going on over
whose family serves up the best meals. It's not the first
time we've run through this game—when you're home-
sick, comfort foods are normally the first things that
come to mind.

"You guys are insane," Del Orbe mumbles through
a mouthful of roast beef. "If you all ever had even one
bite of my dad's infamous sancocho—" His burbling
voice cuts off when I slide into my place at the table
next to Maria.

There's a beat of silence as the group stares into
their plastic trays, and I feel my face heat. I've ruined
it: the only group of people I've ever been able to call

true friends. Me and my stupid, uncontrollable temper. I can't fly away from this. I can't drive away from this. I can't run away from this.

Maria speaks first.

"Del Orbe, please. You haven't tasted cuisine until you've had my grandmother's gumbo," she says loudly. She elbows me and gives me a smile out of the corner of her mouth, and I sag with relief as unshed tears pool in the whites of my eyes.

Amidst the cacophony of protests and rebuttals that Maria's comment inspires—as she knew it would—while Pierre describes the mouthwatering oxtails his grandmother lovingly made for him, and Bianchi counters with stories about his grandmother's gnocchi, I remain silent, letting these familiar voices wrap around me like a cocoon while I berate myself for risking *this* for my own selfish pride.

By the time dinner is over and we burst through the mess hall doors, walking toward McDermott Library for our nightly study session, I need space. I grunt my apologies and peel off toward . . . somewhere else. Anywhere else. My friends—gracious, wonderful human beings that they are—might be over how I acted, but I'm not. It's made me think, and I do my best thinking alone.

What I want is to sit on a picturesque bench and gaze at an awe-inspiring sunset. My hair could swirl out of the confines of its bun, taking romantic shape in the breeze, and a single tear could trail dramatically down my face as I finally grasped the full depth and expanse of the meaning of life.

Instead, I find myself perched on a jagged boulder out behind Mitchell Hall, the only breathtaking thing I'm gazing at being the overflowing dumpster filled with the garbage from dinner. I did luck out on one thing, though. Someone in the kitchen is bumping a pretty solid mixtape. And try as I might, I'm finding it impossible to dive to the melancholy depths I'd hoped for with this peppy, cheery rhythm playing. I try to unpack how I got here as the cassette tape rattles through its unintentional pep talk.

My mind goes blank.

Minutes pass.

I even go so far as to air-drum along to the beat, trying to give my brain a boost. But in the microscopic fragment of time between songs, a burning sensation forms in my chest and begins to crawl up my throat. And before I can lose myself in the next song, its fire engulfs me.

The tears feel like they've come from somewhere so deep that it scares me. Nope, not going to go there. No. Thank. You.

I go into fix-it mode immediately. My head hurts as I force myself to hone in on the reason for all this, or, at the very least, a cohesive list of explanations for why I'm upset, matching each one with a possible solution. But I can't. I'm panicking and spiraling, and the only thing I can pinpoint is that I'm sad and scared. And I don't know why.

What is wrong with me?

"Come on, Carol," I choke out, wiping my now-drenched cheeks with my sleeve.

Flashes of Maria's face. She was so hurt at how I betrayed her confidence in my rashness, but still so kind. The sobs burst out of me at just the thought. A little voice inside gets louder and louder: *You don't deserve such kindness, Carol Danvers. You're a fraud and everyone knows it, Carol Danvers. You're not good enough, Carol Danvers.*

Stubborn to the last, I stand up and try to walk off the pain, as if it were a pulled muscle or a strained hamstring. Pacing back and forth, the choked sobs turn into sharp, angry breaths as I start getting frustrated with my inability to feel better, craft the perfect apology to Maria, and move on.

But I can't move on. Because I don't see a path. The one I'd mapped out all those years ago . . . I'm not welcome on it. Jenks doesn't want me there. They don't want me there.

Why don't they ever want me?

I'm a good pilot. I'm at the top of my class. I've let myself learn and worked on myself. I've waited for the break and held the nose. I've trusted myself and built my character. I've kept my integrity and stopped trying to prove myself all the time.*

"Why isn't it working?" I desperately growl to no one. I sit back down on the boulder and run my hands over my low military-issue hair bun, finally letting my hands drop and burying my face in the cover they provide. I take a deep breath. And another one. And then I let myself sink down into the treacherous quiet of my own mind.

The truth is, my attempts at inducing calm and reassuring myself that I've done everything I can to succeed here are not working, because I've only done all those things just to say that I've done them, I tried, I gave it my all doing it another way, and carry on along the path as planned.

---

*tonight's exchange notwithstanding

Maria's words firework inside my head: *You need to decide how long, and just what you're willing to sacrifice, in order to keep believing that his way is the only way.*

I truly believed that Jenks's way was the only way that I'd be granted access to the fantasy VIP room where no one feels like a fraud. Where everyone gets along and each member is just as important, respected, and beloved as the next.

But that's not the whole truth.

The whole truth is that I thought if Jenks finally opened that door and welcomed me in—letting me onto the Flying Falcons and then allowing me to be one of the first female fighter pilots—then that would mean I was important, whether I believed it about myself or not. I was putting it all on him—my self-validation, my sense of self-worth—even while telling myself my time here so far has been all what I made it to be, that I've been the one in control. I said it, but I didn't believe it.

Jenks's path, even with all of its obstacles and misery, is just flat-out easier. Because as long as I'm on his path, everything is his fault or to his credit. I can blame him for all my pain and frustration and thank him for all my successes, safe in the knowledge that my fate is out of my hands. He'll tell me how to feel and what to do next, and I'll never, ever find myself perched on a stupid rock behind Mitchell Hall completely in the dark about why I'm feeling sad and scared ever again.

On Jenks's path, the answers are like a math problem—I show my work, there's one right answer, and it's so simple I can put a box around it so someone else can tell me if it's right or wrong.

But on my own path, the answer is this rambling mess of half-formed ideas and momentary flashes of insight that can never be corralled into a box—and even if they could, I wouldn't know if they were actually right.

I thought letting myself learn meant knowing enough to pass *their* tests. Learn stuff to prove *them* wrong. Learn so I can (50 percent) rub their noses in it.

But for this to work—for this to *really* work—I've got to be willing—no, I have to be brave enough—to retrace my steps all the way back to that first day when we repeated the Oath of Enlistment, the first day I let Jenks have power over me and the first day my responses told him he mattered—and start over.

My own way.

I sit perched on that rock a little while longer. The music sounds so good and the cold night air feels kind of wonderful. I don't know what I'm going to say to Maria, but I guess that's kind of the point on this new path. Whatever it is, it's going to be honest and come from my heart, and holy smokes, that's far more terrifying than anything Jenks could say or do to me.

At last I wander back to our sleeping quarters. It's still early enough in the night where I open the door to our room thinking Maria will still be in McDermott with Bianchi, Del Orbe, and Pierre. Instead, I find her sitting at her desk surrounded by books and papers. She looks up when I walk in.

I start rambling.

"Hey, so . . . um, I—" This is exactly why people plan what they're going to say, just an FYI. "I thought you'd still be in McDermott."

She shakes her head. "No, I—I wanted to be here for when you came back. I was worried about you," Maria says. And the bursting emotion is back, but this time I know it's the good kind of emotion—even though it feels kinda bad and super uncomfortable.

And I start there.

"I don't know." I take a deep breath. Buy myself some time to form one clear thought in my head. Then I know. I know what I have to say next.

"I love you, too."

"Danvers—" Maria starts.

"That was really hard and I feel super dumb, and I'm not really good at"—I bring my hand to my chest and wave it around limply—"all this."

"Danvers—"

"Please. You're the best friend I've ever had, and I know I totally messed things up by popping off to Jenks, and you tried to warn me. You tried to tell me the whole time that I was cruising for a bruising, but—"

"Danvers!" Maria yells, closing her textbook. I stop talking, plop down on my bed, and slide back against the wall. Maria turns around in her chair to face me. "I need . . . Well, first off I need you to never say 'cruising for a bruising' ever again."

A laugh explodes out of me, the relief and joy catches me totally off guard. "Roger that," I say.

"People mess up. That's not why I was upset with you," Maria says.

"Then why?" I ask.

"It was actually something that Jenks said, which . . . I know—he's the worst—but he was actually repeating Wolff, if that helps at all."

"The 'can I be taught' thing."

"Which sounds a lot like—"

"Let yourself learn," I finish.

"Yep."

"I don't know what it is about those two ideas that scare me. I really don't."

"They scare me too."

"Really?"

"Oh, absolutely. But I think I found a clue."

"What is it?" I ask.

"We're going to go someplace super cheesy, so buckle up," Maria says. I mime strapping into a cockpit and Maria laughs. "I knew you were going to actually buckle up." I pull on the imaginary shoulder harness and give Maria a quick nod and a breezy hang loose.

"Ready," I say.

"What is it that you ultimately want from Jenks?" she asks.

I think back to the unwelcome, but super-enlightening realizations I had sitting on that stupid rock out behind Mitchell Hall. "If he believes I'm good then maybe I can believe I'm good," I say slowly.

Maria nods. "And what happens then?"

"I'll be happy. And finally feel like I belong somewhere. That I'm important. That I matter."

"And what do you feel around me?"

The burning tears are immediate. Maria walks over and sits down next to me. I can't look at her. The tears fall.

"I'm happy. I feel like I belong somewhere. That I'm important. That I matter."

Maria takes my hand. "And do you want to know what I feel around you?"

"Yes," I squeak out through ugly, beautiful tears.

"I'm happy. I finally feel like I belong somewhere. That I'm important. That I matter."

"You do?"

"Yes."

I bark out a laugh and Maria pulls me in for a hug. "So stubborn, Danvers." We sit on my bed and ugly cry for what feels like hours,* but what is actually just a few minutes. When we finally break apart, I feel . . . lighter. Something inside me has shifted, if only by the tiniest of inches.

"We're never going to belong in Jenks's world," I say ruefully.

"No, we're not," Maria agrees good-naturedly, wiping away her tears.

And then smiles break across both of our faces.

"Good," I say.

Maria takes my hand. "He can have it."

---

*days

CHAPTER 16

THE ENVELOPES CONTAINING THE RESULTS OF our private pilot's tests are still just sitting there in a tiny pile on top of Maria's otherwise spotless desk.

Without uttering a word, Maria and I have both gone about our days, careful not to disturb or even acknowledge the envelopes in any way. But the sign-ups to try out for the Flying Falcons close at the end of today. It's time. We need to face this.

"Let's just take them with us down to the track and open them there," I say. Maria's eyes flick over to the envelopes and then back to me. I finish lacing up my shoes and stand. With each step I take toward the envelopes, Maria's eyes get wider.

"Okay, but—" Whatever she is going to say next is cut off by a small yelp as she hops on one foot, the other half-stuck in one shoe, and she nearly trips as she bolts over to where the envelopes are. Seeing Maria's compromised position, I dart forward in one swift motion and beat her to the envelopes, scooping them into my hand and holding them aloft. I laugh at Maria's scowling face.

"Come on. No more thinking. Sign-ups close today. We need to know," I say with the best fake bravado I can muster. Maria drops her arms to her sides and takes a long, resigned deep breath.

We pull on our layers to face the sharp cold outside, and I slide the envelopes into the front pocket of my hoodie while Maria balances on one foot, tying the laces on her other shoe. She's muttering the word *okay* over and over again under her breath.

I flip up my hood and look over at Maria, amused and mildly concerned. "You ready?"

"No."

"Do you honestly think you didn't pass? Like really, honestly?" I ask.

"Do *you* honestly think you didn't pass? Like really, honestly?" she throws back at me.

"Hmph" is all I can manage in reply.

We both stand there in some kind of game of trust-and-believe-in-yourself chicken. Finally, Maria opens the door and sweeps her arm as if to say, *After you*. I stomp begrudgingly out of our dorm room and we both walk down to the track in silence.

Bianchi, Del Orbe, and Pierre are already stretching when we arrive.

"What's wrong?" Del Orbe asks.

"Are you fighting again? I can't take you two fighting again," Bianchi says.

"No, we're not fighting again," Maria says. Their relief is instantaneous.

"Phew," Pierre says, exaggeratedly wiping his brow.

"These came in the mail," I say, producing the two envelopes with a flourish.

"Funny thing about the US Postal Service—envelopes do tend to be delivered," Bianchi says.

I roll my eyes. "They're our test results, smarty-pants." I blow out a puff of air in frustration at the guys' blank faces. "For our private pilot's licenses!"

"Say that ten times fast," Del Orbe says.

"*Prilate pibutts lichent, priveck prabat libben*," Pierre attempts, before crumbling into giggles.

"Pibutts!" Del Orbe barks, clapping Pierre on the shoulder.

"You guys about done?" Maria asks, raising one eyebrow at me. They aren't done. But within seconds we're all laughing and trying to say *private pilot's license* ten times fast—a feat which is apparently impossible. As our laughter dies down, all eyes return to the two sealed envelopes.

"I say just rip 'em open at the same time," Del Orbe says.

"What if one of us passed and the other didn't?" I ask.

"I'd never even thought of that," Maria says, her entire face crumbling.

"That's it. This is ridiculous," Bianchi says, striding over and deftly removing both envelopes from my hands.

Maria and I shout in unison, reaching out to him. As we look on in horror, Bianchi rips open one envelope and then the other. Without a second of drama or making us wait or dragging out this moment to torture us, Bianchi flips both letters around. My entire stomach drops. Time stands still. Everyone is silent.

"You both passed," he says.

Maria and I dive into each other, screaming and hugging and hugging and jumping.

"This is way too much excitement for so early in the morning," Bianchi says, folding up the papers and carefully sliding them back into their respective envelopes.

"Hey, if it gets us out of running . . ." Pierre trails off. "Celebratory cheat day?"

"For real, though," Del Orbe says, raising his hand for a high five. Pierre obliges, and the crack of their hands ripples through the empty track.

Maria and I break apart, and then everyone is hugging and jumping and laughing. Del Orbe pulls me toward him, mussing my hair and telling me how happy he is for me. Pierre throws me into a headlock before telling me in such a serious tone that he's so proud and we worked so hard that his voice cracks, and when I look at him he's taking off his clunky black glasses to wipe away his tears, and now I'm hugging him to comfort him through this emotional time.

And then the whirlpool of hugging spits me out right in front of Bianchi. There's this millisecond of awkwardness and then I lunge into him, lacing my arms around his waist, resting my head on his chest. He pulls me in, wrapping his arms around my shoulders.

I don't feel self-conscious or weird. I just feel like I belong. When we break apart, I look up at him and notice something is . . . off.

"What's wrong?" I ask. He shakes his head and I can see him looking over at Del Orbe, Pierre, and Maria, taking a breath to rally the others and move this morning along or try somehow to push past whatever is bothering him. Takes one to know one.

"We're going to go get a drink of water, you guys go on ahead," I yell, cutting him off. Pierre and Del Orbe groan, having convinced themselves we were all taking the morning off, but Maria corrals them over to the track.

Once the others are out of earshot, I look up at Bianchi, raise my eyebrows. "Shall we?"

"The fact that I'm not thirsty—is that going to stop this little field trip from happening?"

"Nope," I say.

"Fine." He starts toward the water fountain. His pace is fast and unrelenting. In my currently charitable spirit, I let him run-walk in silence, but once we get to the fountain all bets are off. Bianchi bends over and takes a long drink. He wipes his mouth with the sleeve of his hoodie.

When I lower my own mouth to the fountain, the

water is cold and tastes so good, maybe a hundred times better than it did yesterday or the day before. The sky looks clearer than ever, the grass beneath our feet is a brighter color, the birds overhead are chirping louder and in concert.

I laugh at my ridiculousness. I'm so relieved that we passed our private pilot's license tests, it's making me downright giddy. I'm always amazed at my ability to compartmentalize stuff that I'm worrying about. I don't even know I'm doing it until the burden lifts and I feel this lightness I didn't even realize I'd been missing. I stand up and face Bianchi.

"Spill," I say. Bianchi shakes his head as if he's fighting back the words. Pressing his mouth into a single tight line, he puts his hands on his hips and starts to pace. "I don't think I need to remind you how stubborn I am, Danvers."

"No, you definitely do not." I watch Bianchi wrestle whatever is bothering him to the ground. And when he looks up, he finally lets me see his sheer anguish.

"I need you to let me say this whole thing without interrupting."

I nod encouragingly.

Bianchi is quiet for a long time. I take his hand, which for a moment I worry might make him feel weird, but it seems to comfort him. He curls his fingers around mine and finally starts to speak. "You and Maria are our two best fliers. I'm a distant third. I thought it would be way harder to say that out loud, but it actually feels kind of nice to admit it." He squeezes my hand, and the tiniest of tired smiles ekes out. "But I'm still going to make the team, Carol." His face darkens. "And you two aren't."

"We know." My voice is calm and my eyes are locked on his.

"What? But—"

"Maria and I are never going to belong in Jenks's world. She helped me realize that, actually. I've already wasted too much time trying to prove to him that I'm the best. To make him see that I'm valuable and show him that I'm important. We need to find another way. Our own way."

"Then why even try out? Why give him the satisfaction of turning you down?" Bianchi asks, letting go of my hand. A thousand answers race through my head, including the very real possibility that Bianchi is right and we shouldn't even bother, and it dawns on me that this is my new normal. No longer anchoring my self-worth to what Jenks thinks of me has left me sifting through the ruins of whatever I thought I knew about myself. But if I am my own true north, then all I have to do right now is tell the truth and everything will turn out okay.

"I'm not totally sure, but it just feels like the right thing to do, if that makes any sense."

"It does," he says.

"It feels different in here, now," I say, pressing my hand to my chest. Bianchi nods. "I can't explain it."

"You don't have to," he says. I smile, and this calm washes over me. I can trust myself even if I don't have it all figured out. And I'm touched that Bianchi has found himself so tormented by a predicament that isn't even his. The guy has character.

"We'd better get back," I say, looking over at the track. Noble has joined Maria, Del Orbe, and Pierre, and it seems all pretense of an effective morning run has been done away with as they hoot and holler, chasing each other around the track in what looks like some elaborate game of freeze tag. I laugh. With finals closing in and our Recognition ceremony less than a month away, I don't blame them for finding a pocket of time to blow off a little steam.

"You won't think less of me?" I hear this and turn back around to face Bianchi. His face is still ashen.

"For what?"

"That if I do make it onto the team—"

"*When* you make it onto the team," I correct. He shakes off what I've said and continues on as if I didn't interrupt.

"I'll say yes. Then I'll be on Jenks's side," Bianchi says. His voice chokes.

"Hey, Tom. You listen to me." I stare him down. Will him to meet my eyes. "I can wait literally forever, Tom Bianchi. You know I will. This feels like the exact hill I'm willing to die on."

Bianchi laughs and looks up, finally making eye contact. His deep blue eyes are red-rimmed. "Change happens from the inside. If you get on the Flying Falcons, you can begin to . . ." I trail off, searching for the right word.

"You're trying not to say *infect* aren't you?"

"It really is the best word, but—"

"Influence? Is that—?"

I hold up a hand to pause him. "Disrupt. That's the word. We need an inside man to—"

"*Man* being the operative word here."

"You can disrupt Jenks's little outdated fiefdom from the inside and alter it forever. If anyone is the guy for the job, it's you. You're the best man I know, Tom." And just like Maria and me, I watch as Bianchi fights the compliment. Shaking his head, looking at me as though waiting for me to take it back, and then finally he acknowledges it, his face a mixture of reluctance, shame, and exhilaration.

"Thank you," he says simply, his voice a low growl.

But his eyes are bright again, and they flash with that old Bianchi swagger. He bends over and takes one last swig from the water fountain. As we walk back to the track, he speeds up to get to the game of freeze tag, his arms spread wide as if he's soaring. I watch as the pain that was drowning him washes away.

That afternoon, in between classes, Maria and I wend our way through the hallways of USAFA to find the seemingly clandestine office where the Flying Falcons sign-ups are taking place. We ask directions no less than three times, and as the clock ticks down, we finally spot the tiny sign we're looking for. Maria and I look at each other and without a missed beat barrel toward the office.

We pull open the heavy door and step inside. It slams closed behind us, and the civilian woman receptionist behind the counter looks up.

"How can I help you?" She has on a very conservative

navy dress with a sensible black cardigan pulled on over it. Her hair is swept back in a bun, and she's wearing just a swipe of the lightest pink lip gloss. But then I notice it. She has the tiniest hint of neon-yellow eye shadow tracing along her eyelid.

"I like your eye shadow," I say before I can stop myself.

To my surprise, she smiles and leans in toward us. "It's the little rebellions, isn't it, ladies?" she whispers, a sparkle in her eye.

"It certainly is," Maria says with a grin.

"We'd like to sign up to try out for the Flying Falcons, ma'am," I say, a bit louder and more stiffly than intended. I can tell both Maria and I are waiting for Jenks to pop out from behind some old file cabinet with the commandant of cadets in tow—proclaiming, *These! These are the unworthy interlopers I was telling you about, sir! Have them removed from the premises at once!* But Jenks is smarter than that. He wouldn't stop us from signing up. That might send up a flare, or raise some questions as to why we aren't being allowed to try out. He has to let us. Because then, if . . . No, *when* we don't make the team, he can just shrug his shoulders and tell everyone we simply weren't good enough.

The receptionist's face lights up as she hands us a

totally normal-looking clipboard with a pen attached via a too-long chain. The phone rings and she quickly answers it, her entire demeanor changing as she glides through her scripted greeting. Maria sets the clipboard down on the counter. She flips through the pages of names.

"Seventeen people," I say, quickly spotting Bianchi among the rest.

"All vying for just two open spots," Maria murmurs, her eyes darting down the list.

"All men," I say, stating the obvious.

"Not anymore," she says, signing her name. She hands me the pen and I put it to the paper.

"Not anymore," I repeat.

CHAPTER 17

THE WEEK LEADING UP TO THE FLYING FALCONS tryouts, I thought I wouldn't be able to sleep. I thought I'd be withdrawn when we went on our morning runs. I thought I'd be too nervous to eat. I thought I'd be short and clipped with the people in my life, too worried to care about such trivial things as politeness and connection.

I was wrong on all counts.

I slept like a baby. I was loose and happy during our morning turns around the track. I ate absolutely everything put in front of me and went back for more. And I felt more connected with my friends than ever.

And I feel solid now as we suit up for these try-outs. Because, at some point during the gauntlet this last year has been, I learned I didn't have to slice off parts of myself and offer them to other people so they can debate and determine their value. I get to decide. Which means, I will finally meet this day as my complete and powerful self. Whole again.

Jenks is waiting for us on the field, hands behind his back, as are a few of the cadet instructors, including Cadet Instructor Pilot Wolff. The nineteen airmen trying out this morning fall in and listen intently as Jenks walks us through today's proceedings. It's actually pretty straightforward: We wait until our names are called, and then we go up in one of their T-41 Mescaleros and show them what we've got. At the end of the week, Jenks will post the names of the two people who have made the team outside of that weird little office with the cool secretary where Maria and I signed up. And that, as they say, is that.

I notice that most of the people trying out today are upperclassmen. I've seen them around campus. But this'll be the first time I'm going up against them on a level playing field. All of us are competing for the two spots being vacated by graduating first-class cadets.

We're told to sit on the hard wooden benches off to the side in the order in which we will be flying. Bianchi is fifth, Maria is eleventh, and I'm called fifteenth. This is not going to go alphabetically, then. I'm seated between two airmen I've never met, and as the first three names are called, I lean forward and find Maria. She's already got her gaze trained on me. When our eyes meet, she starts mouthing something at me, while I mouth something motivational over at her. We each stifle a laugh beneath our hands that quickly gains steam as part genuine mirth, part an outlet for our considerable nerves. We're trying our hardest not to make a sound, but I see Bianchi look back from the first row, smile, and roll his eyes.

Once our shoulders stop shaking with silent laughter, I gesture to Maria that she should say her thing first. She mouths, *Here we go*. I raise a subtle hang loose in solidarity and mouth the words, *Let's do this*. Affirmations completed, we both settle back into our spots to await our fates.

We all watch closely as the first three airmen are put through their paces. Johnson is among them. He looks unduly confident as he walks toward Jenks and his waiting plane. The two remaining airmen are funneled over to the other two cadet instructors. Realizing that my tryout might just as easily be with Wolff or Cabot as it could be with Jenks is something I hadn't planned on, that should bring relief. But I'm kind of shocked at how little it registers. Showing Jenks what I can do isn't what this day is about anymore.

I don't just know it, now I'm living it.

Jenks, Wolff, and Cadet Instructor Pilot Cabot each walk their airman through extensive safety checks of both the inside and outside of the plane. Jenks encircles Airman Johnson, hands clasped behind his back as always. His cold, yet deceptively beautiful face is arrogant and indifferent as he points and guides Johnson around the plane, dismissively tossing off orders like empty paper cups. Meanwhile, Wolff and Cabot are bending over engines and actively engaging with their airmen, trying to get as complete a picture of their abilities as possible.

Wolff's airman is the first to go up. A long taxi down the runway, a smooth takeoff, and then the little white-and-blue plane with the big USAF on the fin disappears into the big blue. Cabot and his airman are next, taxiing over to the runway. When Wolff's guy returns, it'll be their time to go up. And on and on they'll go until it's my turn.

As I watch each of the airmen have their moment, quite literally, in the sun, it all feels so surreal. I've imagined what this day would feel like all year long. And now that it's finally here, I realize what I'm experiencing is—once again—unlike anything I could have ever dreamed. Skipping the usual exhausting math of gauging how everyone else is feeling and are they thinking this thing about me, and if I can just do that then they'll like me, and if I can convince them of this then they'll welcome me in, and then and only then will I be able to tell you how I'm feeling, is completely freeing. Before this, how I felt entirely depended on how everyone else was feeling. I could never just exist.

But today I'm relaxed, happy even, as I sit and wait for my name to be called. I'm just . . . here. Watching the planes with the warm sun shining on my face. I'm not nervous; I'm not smug; I'm not blazing to prove myself to someone else.

I'm just . . . me.

Bianchi goes up in the second group, and watching him skillfully move around his plane under Wolff's guidance . . . I feel proud. He really is something. I watch as he climbs into the cockpit, straps in, does his checks, and is finally able to have his turn. His takeoff is seamless, and I realize this is the first time I've seen him fly. Maria looks back at me and raises her eyebrows as if to say, *Not bad*. I respond with my own overdramatic faint, still subtle so as not to attract attention from our surrounding peers and cadet officers, and she smirks. I watch as he climbs higher and then higher still, noticing that his flying has this effortless, graceful strength to it that reminds me of Maria's piloting style. A trait that my more "bull in a china shop" ways have not one thing in common with. When Bianchi finally lands, he does so without a bounce. This sends a nervous ripple through the remaining airmen. He was being too modest when he claimed that Maria and I were far superior fliers to him. If he gets a spot, it won't just be because he's a man. It'll be because he's earned it.

Bianchi jumps down from the cockpit, scrapes his hand over his still-shaven head, and salutes Wolff in thanks. Striding across the airfield, Bianchi looks over at Maria and me and gives us a quick, very controlled nod. But I can see him bursting with pride.

Maria and I sit through the next group and then, finally, Maria's name is called. There's a palpable ripple through the group of airmen as one of the two female applicants rises from her seat. She looks back at me and I give her a thumbs-up. She gives me an easy, confident smile, and walks right over to Jenks and salutes. The other two airmen called alongside her have obviously steered clear of Jenks, choosing instead to go up to Wolff or Cabot. Even Bianchi made a beeline for another option, when it was his turn. But not Maria. Where other airmen hesitated or stumbled, Maria is boldly brilliant. This is just another day at hangar thirty-nine for her. She moves through the safety checks without a hint of doubt. She also doesn't take stock of Jenks at all—just enough deference to be properly respectful of a higher-ranking official, but she is impenetrable to his scrutinizing gaze and imposing demeanor. She is calm, cool, and collected—100 percent sure of how well she's doing. By the time she's climbing into the cockpit, a few of the other airmen start shifting in their chairs. I wonder if this makes Maria the first woman to ever try out for the Flying Falcons. It wouldn't surprise me.

Her takeoff is the best yet. It's all precision and power. Her touch is light and confident. I find myself becoming emotional as she climbs high into the sky. We've worked so hard, and there's nothing more beautiful than watching someone who's really good at something finally—and unapologetically—being allowed to do that thing to its full extent.

"She's awesome," the airman next to me says, almost under his breath.

"Yes, she is," I say. He looks over and smiles sheepishly.

"Didn't know I said that out loud," he says. He shields his eyes from the sun, craning his neck so he can watch Maria fly. He's intoxicated. I scan the crowd. Everyone's watching. Riveted.

And just like that, another piece of the puzzle fits into place. Trying out today wasn't about showing Jenks what we can do—trying out today was about showing *everyone* what women can do. So the next time someone like Jenks tries to tell these men that women can't fly, they'll all think back to that one day during Flying Falcons tryouts when they got to see the best flier of the lot with their own eyes . . . and she was an African American woman who wasn't even allowed on the team.

I hope that everyone here today will marinate in the discomfort of that knowledge, and do better when it's their turn to make big decisions. As I've experienced again and again and again throughout the year, letting yourself learn is the most uncomfortable, hardest thing to do. And the most rewarding.

Suddenly, Maria breaks across the horizon doing a slow barrel roll. I actually clap my hand over my mouth in disbelief. I don't know if it's even allowed for an airman to execute a barrel roll in a tryout. Without even thinking about it, I jump to my feet, only to find that everyone else is standing up, too. Airmen are whooping and hollering as she lines up with the runway. Even Cabot and Wolff are grinning, making no effort to calm the others down. As the tires of the plane set down all at once, the group breaks out into another round of applause.

Maria hops down from the cockpit, Jenks emerging shortly after. His face is like stone as Maria salutes him, but I could swear the set of his shoulders has shifted just a bit tighter, as though he's trying to actively push away the effect of witnessing a woman do something *that* cool firsthand.

As she walks away, the wattage from her smile could power the Las Vegas strip. I see her do a little skip and then another one. And then we lock eyes. I can see her mouth tighten and her brow furrow, as she tries to hold back a tidal wave of emotion. She looks to the sky just as the twelfth airman takes off behind her. She shakes her head and looks back over at me with a teary smile. She puts her hand to her heart. I put my hand to my heart, too, as she walks triumphantly off the airfield.

And then it's just me.

The next three names are called—mine the last of the group. I stand, smooth out my flight suit, and walk straight over to Captain Jenks. If Maria can take him, so can I. I salute.

"Airman Danvers," he says. I can see my reflection in his aviator sunglasses. My fishbowl face looks back at me, unruffled and resolute.

"Sir," I say, awaiting orders.

Jenks is dismissive and condescending, but we move through my safety checks relatively painlessly. Jack and Bonnie hammered all this into our heads, and going through these checks feels like second nature at this point. By the time we're climbing into the cockpit, I've completely locked into what's happening because I've done it so many times before. But—and I notice this pretty quickly—in a way harder plane than what awaits me now. That's why Jack and Bonnie had us fly *Mr. Goodnight*. Because if you can fly *Mr. Goodnight*, you can fly anything.

"You're quite impressive, Danvers." I wait. I know that's not all. He can't help himself. "When the plane is still on the ground."

"Thank you, sir," I say, refusing to bite. His jaw clenches. This cockpit is tiny, and Jenks's broad shoulders and giant ego take up most of the room. Sitting shoulder to shoulder with him, I could cut the tension with a knife. The silence expands as I await his orders.

"Start her up," he says.

"Yes, sir," I say, obliging. The engine roars to life and my heart leaps. I curl my fingers around the yoke and taxi the plane over to the runway.

And just like that, it's as though I'm back in *Mr. Goodnight* and this is just another Sunday at Jack and Bonnie's. I know that Jenks is being particularly quiet, and I also know that's not necessarily a good thing, but I chalk it up to the fact that he already knows he's not letting me into the Flying Falcons, so why waste the energy on feedback or, heaven forbid, encouragement? In his mind, my tryout is something to get over with. In my mind, I don't care what he thinks. I just can't wait to fly.

We get clearance from the tower, and I marvel at a radio that I can actually talk to without the need of an air horn. The plane idles and shakes as we wait for the go-ahead. Sitting so close to Jenks in this tiny cockpit, I start to notice more things about him out the corner of my gaze. The tan line where a watch used to be. The piney scent of his aftershave. This super-subtle throat-clearing thing he does every couple of minutes, followed each time with an almost imperceptible head roll. I wonder if that's a tell for something.

In my head, I had built him up to be this all-knowing,

mustache-twirling super villain that held my fate—and the fate of the world—in his hands. But maybe he's just a regular throat-clearing, can't-find-his-watch, aftershave-wearing human, and not a fire-breathing dragon or a monster under my bed.

He's just a man. One man.

Jenks's stomach rumbles from hunger, and I feel his arm tighten next to me. He knows I heard it. He shifts his weight, and the old, worn-in plane seat chirps out a staccato fart noise that echoes throughout the small plane. Holding back the eruption of laughter is taking every ounce of energy I've got.

"Just right there, Danvers," Jenks says. It's a statement that makes absolutely no sense . . . other than to attempt to cover up what is turning into a breathtakingly awkward moment.*

The tower finally crackles through on our radio, telling us we're cleared for takeoff. I confirm and start taxiing down the runway. Faster and faster. Faster and faster. The plane shakes over the rough runway but has nothing on *Mr. Goodnight*. And then in one stomach-dropping swoop—no more shaking.

We. Are. Flying.

---

*for him

And no matter how many times I've done it, the joy surges through my entire body. Jenks tells me to climb to a particular altitude and hit cruising speed. And once again, the blue surrounds me, the misty clouds envelop me, and the weightlessness bewitches me.

"We're at altitude, sir," I say, easing into cruising speed. Jenks is quiet. He stares straight ahead and pulls his hands off his yoke. He takes a long, deep breath. "Sir?" Jenks brings his hands to rest on his legs, his long tanned fingers peppered with little glittering blonde hairs.

"Why are you here, Danvers?" He asks, not looking at me.

"Sir?"

"Even you have the mental capacity to answer such a simple question, Danvers. Shall I repeat it?"

"No, sir." The cockpit begins to close in around me.

"Then?"

"I love flying, sir," I say.

"Do you think your love of flying gives you the right to be here?"

"No, sir. I have the right to be here because I'm the best."

"The best." Jenks's voice drips with sarcasm.

"Yes, sir."

"Turn the plane around, Danvers."

"Sir, I deserve the chance to try out just like everyone else." Even as I speak, I obey his order and turn the plane around.

"You deserve nothing."

"No, you're right." Jenks's body flinches slightly. "I've *earned* the chance to try out just like everyone else."

"I'm confused, Danvers, as to what you think is happening right now? Is this not a tryout?"

"You and I both know that it is a tryout in name only."

"The only thing you and I both know, Airman Danvers, is that you are unsuitable for the United States Air Force in every way."

"No, sir. No—"

Jenks interrupts me. "You're emotional and impulsive. Your bravado is embarrassing. You launch yourself into things without thinking—"

"Isn't that the definition of impulsive?" I can't resist.

"And you're insubordinate."

"Sir—"

"This is my gift to you, Danvers." Jenks grips his hands into tight fists, stretches out his long fingers, and reaches for the panel. "You can thank me later for showing you just how dangerous your recklessness truly is." Jenks reduces the throttle of the plane and lets the nose of the Mescalero fall.

"I'm doing this for your own good, Danvers."

Jenks reduces the power to idle.

The plane shakes and fights. And just as the stall horn blares throughout the tiny cockpit, Jenks takes his hands off the yoke and looks over to me without a word. The nose of the plane dips as the plane begins to gracefully plummet out of the sky. The cockpit enfolds me as Jenks disappears. I tighten my fingers around the yoke. I know what he's trying to do. He wants me to fail, wants me to acknowledge my shortcomings in front of my peers. In some twisted part of him, perhaps he truly does think this is for my own good, and not simply a gross misuse of power.

Unlucky for Jenks, he doesn't know about me and *Mr. Goodnight.*

I let the plane fall.

I wait . . . and wait . . . and wait for the break. Trust myself. My breathing steadies. My eyes focus.

Feel it. Wait. . . . Wait. . . . Hold it. . . .

There. THERE! The break.

And I give the Mescalero full power, pull the nose back to the horizon, right rudder, bring the flaps up, and restore the plane to cruise altitude, successfully performing a standard power-off stall. A bursting swell of pride crashes and streaks through every part of me.

Thank you, Jack.

"All of those things you said about me are true, sir. I'm emotional and impulsive and more than a little cavalier. But I'm also brave enough to let myself learn." I look over at Jenks to find him seemingly composed and aloof. But then I look harder. His face is flushed and his hands are tightly gripping his legs, white knuckles erupting across the tops of his hands.

"You should try it sometime." My parting shot.

Jenks looks over at me.

I pull the plane around toward the airfield and take us home.

Jenks doesn't say another word for the rest of the trip.

CHAPTER 18

"SO HE WAS GOING TO WHAT, JUST LET YOU crash the plane to prove a point?" Del Orbe asks as we walk out of hangar thirty-nine carrying a basketful of steaming biscuits, with Bonnie trailing behind us.

"You can just drop those on the table next to the slaw, Erik," Bonnie says to Del Orbe.

"Straight white bread or nothing!" Jack yells from over by the smoker. Del Orbe looks nervously from Jack to Bonnie.

"It's a Texas thing. You'll be fine, sweetheart," Bonnie says with a wink. Del Orbe looks terrified as he continues over to the table with the biscuits, dropping them onto the surface like hot potatoes and then rushing away, mumbling something about wanting to check out the hangar. Poor guy isn't one for conflict, even the pretend kind.

"No, Jenks was going to save her," Maria says, standing next to Jack and his beloved smoker, a feat of pure ingenuity. Clearly constructed lovingly by Jack himself, it's a delicious crazy quilt of old plane parts that have literally been stitched together by Jack's own steady welding hand. But the real art comes from the mouthwatering smells currently drifting out of its main smokestack.

"Yeah, save me from myself, apparently," I say, holding out a plate as Jack stacks it high with freshly smoked corn on the cob.

"Unbelievable," Maria says, shaking her head in disbelief even though she's relived this story with me dozens of times since it happened.

I walk over to the picnic tables, plate of corn teetering, and Pierre and Bianchi shove aside various salads and a large bowl of macaroni and cheese to make way for the new addition. Jack and Bonnie are throwing a party of sorts for me and Maria, and they insisted that a party is nothing without the whole family. However it started, Bianchi, Del Orbe, and Pierre are our true family here, and Maria and I knew we had to have them celebrating alongside us. Plus, they would never turn down a chance for a home-cooked meal, especially if their mess hall reveries about back-home delicacies were any indication.

"Tom, honey, can you go inside and grab the two pitchers right there on Jack's workbench?" Bonnie says to Bianchi. "One's got sweet tea and the other has fresh-squeezed lemonade. You know what, Garrett, why don't you go on and help him?"

"Fresh-squeezed lemonade?" Pierre asks, his mouth watering.

"Yes, sweetie. Fresh-squeezed lemonade," Bonnie says, pinching his cheeks affectionately. Pierre blushes, but you couldn't wipe the smile from his face if you tried.

"Yes, ma'am," they say. Pierre and Bianchi disappear into the hangar in search of the delicious beverages Bonnie's kind words have promised them, which seem to remind them of home.

"So, now what?" Jack asks, once it's just the four of us.

"Now we find a new way," I say, looking over at Maria. She nods.

"Find a new way to what?" Jack asks.

"A new way to become the first female fighter pilots," I say. Jack and Bonnie share a look.

"Jenks and his Flying Falcons aren't the only game in town," Maria adds.

"Hmm," Jack says as he pulls the meat from the smoker and piles the brisket and pork ribs high onto their respective plates.

"What aren't you saying?" I ask, eyes narrowed. Bianchi and Pierre emerge from the hangar with the pitchers and set those on the table, Del Orbe trailing in their wake.

"I'm just saying there's more than one way to skin a cat, Danvers," Jack says. Just as I'm about to ask what skinning cats has to do with the United States Air Force, Bonnie cuts in.

"That's about as long as I'm okay talking about that man," Bonnie says, herding everyone over to the table. "Now, come on. Let's eat."

Stretching down the entrance of hangar thirty-nine, Jack and Bonnie have set out two long folding tables end to end, surrounded by every kind of chair you can imagine. A red gingham tablecloth flutters in the dusky night air. An old record player plugged into the world's longest extension cord snaking out of the hangar serenades us softly. Old kerosene lamps cast a misty glow over all of us. And standing sentinel is none other than *Mr. Goodnight*, washed and buffed. He's just as much a part of tonight's festivities as the rest of us.

"You gonna take us up in him, sir?" Bianchi asks, gesturing over to *Mr. Goodnight* as we all pull out chairs and scoot them close around the groaning table, momentarily sending the pitchers of sweet tea and lemonade sloshing precariously.

"You think you can handle *Mr. Goodnight*, son?" Jack says, with a wink to Bonnie. Bianchi beams and Bonnie just shakes her head. We all fill our glasses and wait. Bonnie raises her glass.

"To flying," she says.

"To flying," we all say in unison.

And then the ballet of a family dinner begins, the intricate choreography of platters being passed under pitchers refilling cups. A pile of macaroni and cheese is put on a plate just as the secrets to its recipe are told to the eagerly awaiting recipient. Eyes are closed in ecstasy as we experience Jack's brisket, so tender it melts in our mouths. Heads tilt back and laughter peals out over the airfield. We're treated to old war stories, harrowing tales of bravery and sacrifice, and we finally learn how *Mr. Goodnight* earned his name. Bianchi was right. It was not because things went well for anyone else but *Mr. Goodnight*.

At one point in the evening, I look around the table and find myself overwhelmed with a sensation that I can't quite place. But not being able to figure stuff out about myself is something that I've become well acquainted with, so instead of becoming frustrated or scared . . . now I get curious.

I watch as Jack leans down to listen to something Garrett is saying and then throws his head back and laughs, clapping Maria on the shoulder in the process. Erik and Tom lean in as Bonnie tells them a story about a transport mission at the tail end of World War II that went all kinds of wrong. The flickering lanterns. The wafting music. A sip of lemonade and a bite of Bonnie's potato salad.

This is what a family feels like.

This is what it feels like to belong.

This is what it feels like to love and be loved.

"Hey, Danvers. Where are you right now?" Maria asks to my right.

"Hmm?" I ask, floating back down to earth.

"You were very far away," she observes with a smirk.

"I'm just happy," I say, nudging her.

"Me too," she says. We sit in companionable silence.

"So, what do you think Jack meant about there being more than one way to skin a cat?" I ask.

"Aaaand you're back," she says, laughing.

"I am still me, you know," I say, mock-defensive.

Maria takes a sip from her glass. "I mean, they've been trying not to dive into our whole first-female-fighter-pilot plan for a while now."

I nod. "Yeah, but I can see this look in their eye every time we bring it up."

"Bonnie was talking to me about it while we were making her mac 'n' cheese, and, I don't know, it got real." Maria leans over me to get Bonnie's attention. "Bonnie, I was telling Carol about our conversation earlier," Maria says.

"I guess I'm not ready to give up on the dream yet," I say.

"And what dream is that?" Bonnie asks, setting down her cup of sweet tea. She rests her arm on the back of Maria's chair, leaning in even closer.

"The dream of flying combat," I say, my voice smaller than I would have liked.

"So, when you were a little girl, soaring around your

backyard with your arms as wide as they could go—that was about flying combat?" Bonnie asks, velvety smooth.

I pause and think about what she's asking. "No, ma'am," I admit. Maria clears her throat.

"So what was that dream about then, dear?" Bonnie asks.

"To fly . . . just to fly," I say, remembering Noble's drawing and the—seemingly temporary—epiphany that followed, about needing to reclaim the joy I once had for flying.

"And then someone came along and told you that this one kind of flying was the most important kind of flying, and then that's when that dream of yours stopped being a dream and became . . ." Bonnie prompts, her gaze flicking back and forth between Maria and me.

"A way to prove ourselves," we say in droning unison, absolutely stricken that we're back here again.

"A way to prove yourselves," Bonnie repeats, nodding effusively, wrapping her arm around Maria and giving her a little squeeze. "Who you are is for you to define, not them."

"But it's not fair," Maria grumbles, pushing her last bites of food around her plate.

"No, it's not. So now what?" Bonnie asks. Maria

and I look at one another, searching each other's faces for the answer.

"We don't know what our 'now what' is," Maria says.

"We find another way to get there?" I ask.

"No, you find another there, sweetheart," Bonnie says.

"A new there," Maria echoes quietly.

"Girls, listen. I would have been a great fighter pilot," Bonnie starts off.

"Hear! Hear!" Jack interrupts from the other side of the table, raising his glass, apparently listening in. With all those years at the mercy of the air horn, you'd think his hearing wouldn't be quite so sharp.

Bonnie gives him a melty look and he winks back at her, then she clears her throat and continues. "But they took that from me, and once they did that, I wasn't about to let them take flying away from me, too."

"If it's about flying, then make it about flying," Jack says.

"And stop making it about only flying combat," Bonnie adds.

"Because that way lies madness," Jack finishes.

The rest of the table has quieted now to follow this exchange. "Shakespeare?" Pierre asks.

"'Oh, that way madness lies,'" Bonnie muses.

"*King Lear*," Pierre says to a confused Bianchi and Del Orbe.

"I feel so stupid right now I can't believe it," Bianchi says.

"So, just like any other day, then," Del Orbe says. And the whole table howls and hoots as Bianchi raises his glass and laughs, breaking the gravity of the moment.

A new there. I roll it over and over in my head, taste it on my tongue. But how do we find it?

"Honey, can you help me with the cherry pie?" Bonnie asks. Del Orbe stands up immediately, and upon doing so it becomes clear pretty quickly that he wasn't the honey she was referring to.

"I'm her main honey, son," Jack says with a mock growl, clapping him on the shoulder.

"I mean, I can help, too," Del Orbe says following them inside the hangar.

"A new there," I say out loud. I can't get past it.

"You ever think about helicopters?" Pierre asks. We all groan, and he throws his hands up in protest. "What? They're awesome. You guys know I saw the Silver Eagles back when I was a kid, and—"

"They're disbanded now, but they made me want to fly," we all complete in unison.

"Okay, verrrrry funny," Pierre says, grabbing a biscuit from the basket.

"I've thought only about flying combat for a very long time," I say.

"Me too," Maria adds.

"Ugh, this is that 'let yourself learn' thing again," I say, realizing it.

"What 'let yourself learn' thing?" Bianchi asks.

"Driving to USAFA on that very first day I got stopped by this state trooper. I was speeding and maybe being a bit 'reckless,' but this guy in a Jaguar had—"

"Nope, I've got it. You don't have to tell me another word. I'm pretty sure I know exactly what happened," Bianchi says. His eyes twinkle as he points his fork at me. "Let me guess. Something about you throwing yourself into the middle of a situation that had nothing to do with you except for the fact that you couldn't stand by while someone powerless was being mistreated?"

"Okay, fine. That's exactly what happened," I say.

"Yeah, I have met you, you know."

I wave my hand at him dismissively. "Anyways. The state trooper let me off with a warning and I thought it was just going to be this kind of ha'ticket—"

"Nope. Not a word," Bianchi says.

"Ha'ticket. Like a ha'penny, but this time, instead of half a penny, it means half a ticket. Ha'ticket," I say, unblinking.

"I like it," Pierre says, plucking yet another biscuit from the basket in the middle of the table. The guy could really put it away.

"Maria, please back me up on this," Bianchi says. Maria throws her hands up in surrender. Bianchi deflates.

"So tell me more about this . . ." We all wait. Bianchi lets out a long weary sigh. "Ha'ticket."

"She wrote on the ticket 'Let yourself learn.' And it's been this sort of thing for me ever since."

"I mean, it's kind of haunted you," Maria points out.

"In a good way, but yeah."

"A ha'ticket has haunted you, but in a good way," Bianchi says slowly, his face screwing up as he tries to understand.

"See, I can be very stubborn," I say.

"What?" Maria pretends to faint.

"No!" Bianchi gasps.

"You don't say!" Pierre blurts out, clapping his hands to his head comically.

I roll my eyes. "I know that's no great secret. But I guess I didn't . . . *wouldn't* see the bad parts of sticking to your guns," I say. "I didn't see that as long as I kept myself locked away in my own sense of what's right and wrong, and what I believed I needed or deserved, I would be closed off to everything else."

"I definitely get that," Bianchi says.

"I was wrong about a lot of stuff," I say, making particularly pointed eye contact with Bianchi.

"Me too," he says, holding my gaze.

"But as misguided as I've been at times, it's still weird to think I could be wrong about the flying-combat thing," I say.

"I don't know another there," Maria says quietly.

"Not yet," Pierre corrects her.

"Let yourself learn," Bianchi says, circling his hand around.

"In order to find the new there . . ." I trail off.

"You have to let yourselves learn," Bianchi finishes.

"Right," I say.

At that moment, Jack, Bonnie, and Del Orbe emerge from the hangar with the cherry pie. Bonnie sets the pie down in the middle of the table, along with a gallon of fresh-churned vanilla ice cream.

"Before we dig in, Bonnie and me . . . we wanted to give y'all something," Jack says, digging into his pocket.

"From a couple of old fliers to you," Bonnie says. All five of us melt as one.

Jack pulls out five shiny silver dollars from his pocket. He drops three into Bonnie's hand and she hands one each to Bianchi, Del Orbe, and Pierre. Jack walks around the table and drops one shiny silver dollar into the palm of my hand and then one into Maria's.

"They're from the year you underclassmen were all born," Jack says, as we study the coins.

"You carry them with you for good luck," Bonnie says, her eyes flicking skyward.

Jack pulls his own silver dollar from his pocket, as does Bonnie. They pass them around.

"They're rubbed smooth," Del Orbe says, brushing his thumb along the flattened surface of Bonnie's coin.

"Well, that year we needed a whole lot of good luck," Bonnie says, pulling Jack in close.

"Think it was more than good luck," Maria says.

"No, darlin'. Sometimes luck was all it was," Jack says.

"A lot of good men and women didn't make it home," Bonnie says. The table falls silent.

"Thank you," Bianchi says, holding his coin with pure wonder. Del Orbe and Pierre offer their own choked thanks, pocketing their coins with newfound reverence.

"For everything," I add on.

"For so much," Maria says, almost to herself.

"Whatever happens next, you must always remember who you are. Not what they say you are," Bonnie says.

"Now before you softies drown in your own tears, let's eat this cherry pie," Jack says gruffly. I could have sworn I saw him wipe something out of the corner of his eye, but pressing the issue would be pointless—if I called him out, he'd promise it was a bug, or a speck of dirt.

Good old Jack.

"Who wants à la mode?" Bonnie asks.

All of our hands shoot up.

CHAPTER 19

WE FIND OUT WHO MADE THE FLYING FALCONS this Friday, but standing between here and there is one thing: Recognition.

When I first heard about Recognition, I thought it would be like a graduation ceremony. An end-of-the-year event highlighting our achievements that concludes with the Recognition dinner, where we're finally given our prop and wings.

And I was *technically* right.

Recognition is an end-of-the-year event that highlights our achievements, but instead of an afternoon filled with frilly dresses, droning renditions of "Pomp and Circumstance" and long, boring speeches, it's three packed days of physical and mental exertion that makes Basic look like summer camp.

Finals are over, classes have ended, and now, back in our squadrons, day one of Recognition begins. And there's Chen and Resendiz waiting for us, and suddenly, I'm back at Basic and it feels like it was yesterday and eternities ago all at the same time.

We quickly fall into our retreat formation along with the other squadrons. As I stand there—shoulders back, eyes forward—today slides down over me like an old T-shirt recovered from the bottom of my closet after months of thinking it was long gone.

I've spent this year putting everything I thought I knew under a microscope only to discover that, up close, nothing was as it appeared to be. The *who*, *what*, *where*, *when*, *why*, and *how* of my life became one big *huh?*

But this? Standing in retreat formation shoulder to shoulder with Maria and Del Orbe with Bianchi and Pierre just one row back feels so good. So comfortable and familiar and right. I can do this. With all the endless questions this year has raised, it feels incredible to sink into the simplicity of a learned routine, to turn off my brain for a moment and let my muscle memory do the hard work. You want me to march in formation and salute and be yelled at and drill and left-face and right-face and present arms and consistently hit that perfect twelve inches between my feet at parade rest? I would be happy to, as I'm pretty sure no one is going to pop out from behind Resendiz and question whether or not me lining up my thumb with the seam of my pants has any deeper meaning than just me lining up my thumb with the seam of my pants.

These next three days are about following orders and working as a team with the rest of my squadron, plain and simple. And I am very excited to do both of those things to the best of my ability.

"Squadron, tench-hut," Chen yells. And it's music to my ears.

Chen and Resendiz move us through day one of Recognition about as delicately as they ran us through First and Second Basic. With each day getting harder and harder, day one just wets our whistles more than knocks us into the ground.

I catch glimpses of our group throughout the day and marvel at what a difference a year makes. Our morning runs, our study sessions, every time we've been put through our paces—I can see the effects of all of it as we move seamlessly around the field.

I feel like a completely new person since that very first day as a "rainbow," save one very important thing: I still want to look around and squeal, *Can you believe we're finally here?! Isn't it great?!*

I love that through all of it—even though sometimes it can be a bit elusive—I retained that joy.

As day one comes to an end, we grunt our goodbyes to Bianchi, Del Orbe, and Pierre after dinner, and Maria and I crawl under our covers before completely conking out. Even the bone-deep exhaustion feels good. Being too tired to think about whatever Maria and my "new there" is, is just the respite I need.

I sleep like the dead, and when the alarm sounds for our morning run, I'm positive it's still the middle of the night. My eyes flutter open and I see Maria stirring in her bed. And it hits me that this is almost over. The number of days that I'll be in this dorm rooming with Maria can be counted on one hand.

"Why are you creepily staring at me?" Maria says, her voice still froggy with sleep, sitting up and setting her feet on the floor.

"Okay, yes I was staring at you, but I would argue that it wasn't creepy so much as wistful," I reason, crossing the room to turn on the light. Maria shrinks away from the harsh fluorescence that floods our little room.

"Wistful," she repeats, blinking her eyes and adjusting to the artificial brightness.

"Wistful. Because it just hit me that we're not going to be roommates for that much longer," I say, pulling my running clothes out from my drawers and picking up my sneakers.

"I've been sad about that for weeks, and you're telling me it just hit you right now?" Maria rubs her eyes and opens her mouth wide in an epically long yawn.

"No, I mean—"

"I'm a better friend than you, Danvers," she says, grabbing her toiletry bag. She goes to open our dorm room door.

"You're a better everything than me, Rambeau," I say. She turns back around and smiles, but before either of us can crumble into a fit of hysterics, Maria disappears out the door.

I finish getting dressed just as Maria returns from the bathroom and I'm sitting on my bed with one shoe on and one shoe listlessly drooping in my other hand, literally frozen in thought.

"Oh no," Maria says automatically.

"I'm going to give a speech," I pronounce, standing. My one shoe is still in my hand.

"A short speech or a Danvers speech?" Maria asks, unable to keep from smiling.

I solemnly hold up one hand for silence. "I know we started out as roommates and then became friends, but I would be honored if—" Nope. Painted myself into a bit of a speech corner there.

I try again. "I think of you as my sister." My voice is loud and robotic, as if I somehow shattered one of my eardrums while Maria was in the bathroom. I'm now inexplicably holding up my one shoe like it's a scroll overflowing with a list of our inalienable rights. Maria is quiet. I clear my throat. "That's it. That's my speech." And then I bow. I have no idea why. I plop down onto my bed and start putting on my other shoe.

"I think we got stuck with each other for life the first day we flew *Mr. Goodnight*. Do you remember that?" Maria walks over and sits down next to me on my bed.

"Every second," I say.

"You'd just flown him for the first time, and I was standing outside of hangar thirty-nine with Bonnie, reliving every moment of our hop as we waited for you," Maria says.

I nod. "I remember."

"You jumped down out of that cockpit and ran over to me and—"

"I hugged you," I say. Maria shrugs. A stream of tears traces down my cheeks.

"I've considered you my sister from that moment on," Maria says, but her casual tone belies her eyes that are welling with tears.

I swallow, hard. "I have no idea what I did to deserve a friend like you."

"You don't just deserve a friend like me. You've earned a friend like me," she says.

I press my lips together in an attempt to control my emotions. It doesn't work. Of course it doesn't work. I should know that by now.

"A side hug would be weird, right?" I ask.

"We crossed the Weird Rubicon months ago, Danvers," Maria says, leaning over and pulling me in close.

"I've been stuck in the Weird Rubicon for years," I whisper in her ear, and Maria barks out a laugh.

Several minutes later, Maria and I run onto the field.

"You're late," Bianchi remarks.

"We were crying and hugging," I say with a grin.

"I knew that's what girls do in their rooms when we aren't around," Del Orbe mutters, almost to himself.

"I think we should take today easy. The second day of Recognition is the hardest, and then we have the Run to the Rock tomorrow," Maria says.

"Which is five miles," I add.

We all begin stretching out our tight calves and arms, still sore from yesterday's exertions. "So are you guys going to tell us why you were crying and hugging?" Bianchi asks.

"I'm just going to miss this, is all," I say, looking around at everyone and spreading my arms wide, as though I can gather the whole group close with one swoop of my arms.

"Oh no," Pierre says, resting his hands on his hips and looking up to the sky as he blinks rapidly. "I've been dreading this moment." He paces around the field, pressing his lips together and shaking his head. "Knew I was going to get emotional." Our little softie.

"Danvers made a speech," Maria says, sitting on the field and starting her stretches.

"We've got another three years, Danvers. This"—Bianchi gestures to all of us—"isn't going anywhere."

"I know that up here." I put my finger to the side of my head. And then I bring my hand down to rest on my heart. "But not here." I look around at everyone. "Too cheesy?" Maria beams over at me and shakes her head no. Pierre is a wreck at this point, and Del Orbe has brought the collar of his shirt up over his face to hide his tears.

"No, definitely not cheesy," Bianchi says, his mouth pressed into a hard line. "I get it." We all look at the ever-steely Bianchi, waiting for him to crack. Not a flicker.

"What?" he barks at us. We wait.

"I'm not going—" Bianchi's face flushes. "Let me just get through the next two days. I can't . . . It's too much. I have to put a pin in"—he brings his hand to his heart—"all this. Just for the next two days and then"—his voice cracks "—maybe I'll start to be able to come to terms with how much each of you has meant to me."

"Two days," Pierre says, sniffling.

"When we get to the top of Cathedral Rock tomorrow, I promise to be the emotional mess that you weirdos apparently require of your friends," Bianchi says with an exhausted laugh.

"We need a group photo," Maria proclaims.

"Of all of us bawling our eyes out? No, thank you," Bianchi says.

"I'm getting that group photo," Maria insists, standing. Discussion closed. We pull ourselves together and start our daily run around the track.

Day two of Recognition is a series of four of the most grueling, brutal courses any human being has ever thought up. It's the Course to End All Courses. We start at 7:00 a.m. and go nonstop until 4:00 p.m. I remember very few details except being yelled at while I carry one of my fellow cadets on my back throughout one course. Being yelled at as I hold my weapon over my head for what feels like hours. And being yelled at as I run up and down bleachers, around the field, up the field, and down the field. We take a tour of the Academy, and at each memorial perform innumerable sit-ups, pull-ups, and push-ups. I'm going to have counting nightmares tonight for sure, before being startled awake by an otherworldly *Tench-hut!* At some point after lunch I discover a new level of exhaustion deep within myself, and as I'm being yelled at while I'm lifting and flipping a giant tire across the field over and over again, I find a new reservoir of strength I didn't know was within me. And that's saying something, after the year I've had.

Limping away from the mess hall after dinner, my legs and arms are so beyond sore that it's easier to pinpoint where I'm not aching, rather than where I am: The good news is, my earlobes appear to be utterly pain-free at the moment.

227

As our group walks toward our dorms, I realize what day it is.

Friday.

I'm shocked that it took all day for me to realize, but at the same time I understand my brain's need to compartmentalize so I could get through today's activities. But now, with full stomachs and drooping eyelids, I know we can't avoid it—we have to go see who Jenks let onto the Flying Falcons.

I don't know what I'm expecting to see. I've been waiting for this moment all year. What was once such a clear bull's-eye of a goal has expanded so far beyond just getting onto the Flying Falcons. In fact, that original objective seems almost too small now. And I'm not delusional enough to think that Jenks will ever allow Maria or me on the team anyway. But maybe there's still the tiniest sliver of hope way down underneath that someone else was watching. Someone higher up who'd confront Jenks and challenge him about his reasons for not letting the two best fliers onto the team. I don't know. Maybe I am delusional.

"You guys." I stop in my tracks, bringing Del Orbe up short behind me with a surprised *oof*. "The Flying Falcons. The list should be posted by now."

"Do you need us to go with you, please say no," Pierre says, looking like he's about to curl up right where he is and go to sleep.

"We're so tired," Del Orbe adds. His voice is a childlike whimper.

"Go to bed, you sissies," Bianchi says with a light laugh.

"You're so meeeeean," Pierre says. But nonetheless he and Del Orbe continue toward the dorms, holding each other up in the process.

And then there were three.

"Let's go look at this list before all my muscles seize up," Bianchi says with a slight hitch in his step. We wend our way through the hallways, toward the most hidden office on campus. This time, it's so much easier to find, since it's been burned into my memory. We come to a stop about a foot away from the little room.

"I'm nervous," I say.

"What if none of us got on?" Bianchi asks.

"I was just thinking that," Maria says.

"How did that possibility just slip right through all our elaborately planned scenarios?" Bianchi asks, laughing.

"We really do need to work on that," I agree.

We are quiet. And then as if we all feel it at the same time, we walk the few steps it takes to view the list of two names posted outside the office.

FLYING FALCONS
Bianchi, Tom
Johnson, Bret

"Bret Johnson?" Bianchi asks in disbelief, skipping over any joy at all at his own name being up there as well.

"There were way better upperclassmen than Johnson," Maria says, crossing her arms across her chest.

"I would say it doesn't make sense, but . . ." I trail off.

"Yeah, but this is a giant overcorrection," Bianchi finishes.

"Even for Jenks," Maria says.

"Well, it's sending a very clear message," I say.

"That he's completely out of touch and on his way out?" Maria asks, her voice clipped and frustrated.

"Fingers crossed," I say.

We stand in stunned silence.

"I know it's dumb, but a part of me still thought . . ." Maria says, before trailing off, as though her pride can't bear for her to complete the sentence. But we know what she wants to say.

"Me too," Bianchi says.

"Me too," I say.

"He could have changed the world," Bianchi says. And just like that our bigger goal comes into focus.

Find a new there.

"I guess we'll just have to do it ourselves, then," I say. Bianchi and Maria nod, and the frustration melts away. Newly focused. Newly committed. A new goal. A new purpose. After several minutes, Maria finally breaks the intense silence.

"Congratulations," Maria says to Bianchi.

"Thank you," he says. But his voice is flat.

"You're going to do so great," I say, my tone almost cajoling. I am genuinely happy for Bianchi in this moment—he earned it. And I want him to feel it, too.

"Thanks," he says. An easygoing, wan smile, not even close to what the situation warrants. I narrow my eyes.

"You're putting a pin in this too, aren't you?" I ask.

"Oh, one hundred percent," Bianchi says.

"Saving it for the top of the rock?" Maria asks.

Bianchi grins. "Might as well."

CHAPTER 20

IT'S THE FINAL DAY OF OUR FIRST YEAR AT USAFA.

Maria and I stand at attention in the center of our dorm room, dressed in our blues. This last Saturday morning inspection is excruciating, but mercifully brief. And in under five minutes, we're getting re-dressed and rushing out to meet everyone else before the Run to the Rock. My body is on autopilot, numbed by the physical challenges it's endured. Even my earlobes have succumbed at this point.

As we fall into formation, a brand-new feeling is infusing all of us. It's a very controlled, barely tamped-down exhilaration. We're like bubbles being blown out of a little plastic wand, whizzing and darting throughout the USAFA campus.

As we stand and wait under a pennant emblazoned with our squadron number, the rumblings and the butterflies and the energy builds and builds and builds as the minutes tick away until we can start our five-mile run to the top of Cathedral Rock.

I look over at Maria, and I can tell she feels it. A smile plays at the corners of Pierre's mouth, and Del Orbe sways ever so slightly back and forth to music that only he can hear. I scan the crowd for Bianchi. I find him. He's so still, it's as if he's spellbound. His face is aggressively dispassionate. He won't look at me. I see him take a long breath, shake something off, and then clench his jaw tight as he resituates himself.

Chen and Resendiz come around to each one of us, yelling inspirationally in our faces. They're trying to get us ready for this last day, which feels so perfect it almost makes me cry. When Chen finally comes around to me, I don't know whether to be emotional or terrified.

"Airman Danvers!" Chen yells.

"Yes, ma'am!"

"You have shown us you are capable of great things!" Chen yells.

"Thank you, ma'am!"

"Do you know what's more important than showing us you are capable of great things?" Chen asks. My mind is a dizzying montage of everything that's happened over the last year. Unable to pinpoint one.

"No, ma'am!" I yell.

"That you showed yourself you're capable of great things!" Chen yells back.

"Yes, ma'am!" I yell.

"Do you know how capable you are, Airman Danvers?" Chen yells.

"Yes, ma'am!" The words pour out of me without hesitation.

"You've made me proud, Airman Danvers," Chen says, her voice dipping slightly. My eyes flick to hers and there's a millisecond of recognition between us. We've both weathered Jenks's oozing dismissiveness and yet here we are—thriving.

"Thank you, ma'am!" I yell back. And she gives me the coolest, most under-the-radar wink before she moves on to the next cadet.

Heartfelt motivational eruptions explode all around. I let them wash over me. Resendiz yells at Maria about her unflagging integrity. Chen yells at Del Orbe about his resilient determination. Chen yells at Pierre about his courageous kindness. Resendiz yells at Bianchi about his steady leadership.

By the end of our final formation as fourth-class cadets, we're all stock-still emotional wrecks. Except Bianchi, of course.

And then one by one, we're given the all clear to start making our way, as a squadron, up to Cathedral Rock. The pace is slow, and with each step the lingering soreness in my body seems to disappear and be replaced by this effervescent pride. I am being propelled to the top of this mountain by unadulterated joy.

I did it.

No.

We did it.

I look around at our squadron. And then I scan the hill in front of me. So many squadrons. All these people. We did it. I am no longer on my own. I am part of a *we*. I am part of the Long Blue Line.

I've earned the right to belong in these people's lives. Because first I was brave enough to belong solely to myself. By surrendering my need for trophies and validation, I've been given the greatest thing anyone could ever have: purpose.

It's weird now to think that for so many months, the only thing I wanted from this year was to make the Flying Falcons—which reminds me how little I thought of myself. My teeny tiny goals matched my teeny tiny opinion of myself.

Maria and I once thought we'd never fit into Jenks's world, and I thought that was some great tragedy. But now I know differently. We don't fit into Jenks's world because we've become way bigger than anything he could ever imagine.

It's scary and messy, and there aren't any definitive answers, but the view from up here is beyond anything we could have found if we were trapped inside Jenks's suffocating definition of who he thought we were.

Out here—in this wild, sprawling big blue sky—we are finally free to be who we really are.

Powerful. Curious. And beautifully, recklessly human.

I'm dragged out of my reverie by the not-so-distant sounds of cheering and yelling coming from the top of the rock. It feels like my chest is going to explode as we turn the final corner. Squadron after squadron reaches the top, and one by one they dissolve into an exhausted outpouring of everything the cadets have been holding in over the last year.

Our squadron makes it to the top of the rock, and all at once Pierre, Del Orbe, and Maria mob me. Then our little mob is gulped up by our squadron's bigger mob, and we quickly become this whirling, out-of-control squadron/blob, jumping and hugging on the top of Cathedral Rock, which looks out over Colorado Springs. We finally break apart and everyone from our squadron goes to the other squadrons searching for friends. Which is when we realize we can't find Bianchi.

We scan the landscape. We all see him at once.

Bianchi is standing on the fringes of the celebrations, holding a small white Polaroid camera with a rainbow stripe tracing down its face in one hand as the other unsuccessfully swipes away the streaming tears that run down his cheeks. He sees us notice him and just shakes his head and laughs.

"This is all your fault," he says, sniffling, as we lunge toward him in one unified, rolling wave. He wraps his arms around all four of us and pulls us in, his body shaking with the now-unpinned lava flow of emotions. We hold each other for what feels like hours, which for a bunch of non-huggers* is well beyond any of our comfort zones.

When we finally break apart, I notice that we're all still kind of holding on to some part of one another.

---

* except for Pierre, of course

A linked arm here, a hand being held and an arm wrapped around a shoulder there.

"Where'd you get the camera?" Pierre asks.

"I've had it." We collectively give Bianchi a look of incredulity. "My mom sent it to me a while back because she felt I wasn't properly communicating with her about my USAFA experience," he says, his face coloring.

"How did you get it up here?" Maria asks.

"Very carefully," he answers with an arched eyebrow.

Looking out over the crowds and squadrons also taking their group photos and enjoying the (almost) end of Recognition festivities, we notice Noble sitting with a few of the people in her squadron. We call her over and ask if she'd be okay with taking a photo of all of us. Five times.

"Five times. The same photo?" She asks.

"Five photos. Five of us," Pierre explains.

"It almost seems that what you need is something like a photocopier," Noble says, hitting the words *photo* and *copier* with particular disdain.

"Can you do it or not?" Maria asks, impatient.

"Yes, I am physically and intellectually capable of taking a single picture five times," she says.

"There are literally hundreds of people up here! How have we landed on Noble being our only option?"

I groan to no one in particular, a smile on my face.

"Because you love me," she says, holding out her hand for Bianchi's camera.

"God help us, but we do," Del Orbe says.

"Now get into whatever pose you want to hold for five totally separate pictures," Noble says, dryly.

Maria stands in the middle of all of us, unmoving. Our moral center. Our anchor. Pierre and Del Orbe stand on one side of her, draping their arms around each other's shoulders like long-lost brothers. Bianchi and I settle on Maria's other side. The tallest of the group, Bianchi takes a small step just behind me. I lean back into him and he rests his hand on my shoulder. Maria holds out her hand and I squeeze it tightly inside mine.

And one by one, with a long-suffering sigh in between each, Noble takes five pictures. One for each of us.

If anyone were ever to see all five photos sequentially, what they would show would be a group of friends smiling wider and wider as we become completely overwhelmed with tears. Whoever gets that last photo will be the proud guardian of what could look like the saddest moment in all of our lives.

Or the happiest.

We decide not to say good-bye. None of us can handle it. Instead, we all tell each other we'll see them around, catch them later, as though it's the end to any other day.

I save Bianchi for last.

"See you in the fall," I say. My face is smushed into his chest as he wraps his arms tightly around me.

"See you in the fall," he says.

"I've never been happier to be wrong about someone than I was about you," I say.

"Me either," he says, hugging tighter.

The trek down the hill is a quiet one. We're all reflective and exhausted. So comfortable with one another, our bodies bump and thread through each other's all the way down.

We take our showers and get dressed for our Recognition dinner in Mitchell Hall. The roar of applause as each one of us is called up to receive our prop-and-wings pin disappears into the background as I try to soak up every last moment.

When it's finally my turn, I walk up to Chen and Resendiz and receive the prop-and-wings pin that I'll proudly wear on my flight cap. I hold it in the palm of my hand. It's heavier than I thought it would be, its cold metal dense and solid. I close my hand around it and walk back to my table, floating on air.

At the end of the ceremony, Maria and I head back to the dorm. We're going to leave tomorrow, but before we head off in our different directions, we've made a plan to do one last errand first thing in the morning. Just the two of us. This is a completely transparent plan to put off saying good-bye to each other until the very last minute. A completely transparent plan that we're both totally okay with 100 percent.

"Danvers. Rambeau. A moment." A man's deep voice just behind us.

We turn around to see none other than the commandant of cadets, Brigadier General Whalen. I've never seen him this close before. White haired and distinguished, being in his presence is immediately humbling. His uniform is overrun with decorations and ribbons that tell the story of a highly esteemed career. I'm struck dumb. How does he even know our names? Maria and I snap to attention and salute. The stream of cadets happily going back to their dorms give us a wide berth, quieting briefly as they pass by this unlikely little triangle we've formed.

"I was lucky enough to be on hand for this year's Flying Falcons tryouts. Haven't seen a barrel roll like that since my days in the Thunderbirds, Rambeau." I feel Maria's body tighten next to me.

"Thank you, sir," she says. Her tone is even, but knowing her as I do, I can hear how her voice is tight with disbelief and excitement.

"Where did you learn that?" He asks.

"Bonnie Thompson, sir?" It comes out like a question.

"Oh, sure. I know Bonnie. She flew me to work during Vietnam," Whalen says.

"Yes, sir."

He turns to me. "And was that a power-off-stall that Captain Jenks put you through up there, Danvers?"

"Yes, sir."

"It was well done, Airman."

"Thank you, sir."

"Did Bonnie teach you as well?"

"No, sir. Jack Thompson taught me."

"Please tell me that he didn't take you up in that old Stearman of his," Whalen says, laughing.

"Yes, sir. He did," I say, allowing myself a tiny smile.

"Remind me again what he calls that old plane?"

"*Mr. Goodnight*, sir," I say. And Brigadier General Whalen barks out a laugh. Maria and I sneak a quick glance at one another.

"*Mr. Goodnight*," Whalen repeats with a chuckle.

"We both flew him, sir," I add.

"You learned a slow barrel roll on that old Stearman?" he asks Maria.

"Yes, sir." Whalen is quiet for a long time. Maria and I wait. Unmoving.

"Have you ever thought about becoming test pilots?"

"No, sir," Maria and I answer in unison.

"Let me make a call. I'll be in touch with you both," Whalen says, before dismissing us and going on about his way.

Maria and I look at each other, speechless. Someone was watching.

"Test pilots," Maria breathes.

"I didn't even . . . I hadn't even . . ." I stammer.

"Becoming a test pilot is a huge deal, Danvers," Maria squeals.

"It's beyond—" It hits me. In our all-consuming quest to become part of the Flying Falcons, we had overlooked this alternate route—different, not better or worse, just different. And something that, in this moment, appears to be entirely achievable. I shake my head in disbelief. "It's our new there."

"Our new there," Maria repeats.

"Wow," I say. It's such a weirdly simple word, but it perfectly encompasses the gobsmacked awe I'm currently experiencing.

We start walking again. "Before we totally freak out over the test-pilot thing, can I just point something out? He said Bonnie flew him to work during Vietnam, right?"

"Yeah, why?"

"Whalen's career has some super-secret stuff in it, and if she flew him to work during that time—"

"Yeah, but she told us she flew transport," I say.

"Rumor has it—and this is just from my pop, so take it or leave it—but he says that it was the CIA who flew guys like Whalen to work during Vietnam," Maria says. She stops walking and turns to me.

"Danvers! What if Bonnie was a spy?"

"What? That's—" And then I think about it for one half a second. "Yeah, you know what? That makes sense."

"Doesn't it?!"

Maria and I laugh, and continue walking in silence.

"Bonnie Thompson was totally a spy," Maria says to herself.

" 'Whatever happens next, you must always remember who you are. Not what they say you are,' " I say, repeating what Bonnie said to all of us the night of their barbecue.

"She never let anyone tell her who she was," Maria

says as we walk back to our dorms for the very last time.

"Ever," I say, reverently.

Maria and I talk nonstop for what feels like hours. No silence lasts beyond a couple of seconds. I don't know if we're nervous or in denial or excited about this test-pilot thing, and amazed at Bonnie Thompson, and full of love and pride and friendship. Or if it's all of the above. But as I toss and turn throughout the night, the worries and doubts start to flutter around inside my head again. I turn onto my back and stare up at the ceiling, a shaft of blue early-morning light breaking across our now-unadorned dorm room, our assorted belongings packed into duffle bags. I let out a long exhale and remember everything that I've learned this past year. And the worries and doubts continue to flutter around inside my head, but this time I don't fear them.

Because it's okay to be scared. It's okay to not know. It's okay to let myself learn.

Because that's how we're going to change the world.

I flip onto my side, tuck my pillow into the crook of my arm, and finally fall asleep.

Maria and I set off down the hill early the next morning in my car. Our windows are down, the radio is loud, and we're officially done with our first year at the United States Air Force Academy.

The world awaits. But first, our errand.

The drive is relatively painless, and Maria and I arrive at our destination way ahead of schedule. We climb out of the Mustang and I walk back to the trunk, open her up, and pull out all of today's necessities. I walk back to the front of the car.

"Be careful. It's old and unreliable," I say, handing Maria the old canteen filled with the most caffeinated tea I could get my hands on. It's warm now, so we don't need the plaid blanket, but I hand it to her anyways. It's tradition.

"They do still make canteens available for purchase, you know," Maria says, scrambling up onto the hood of my old Mustang.

"Yeah, but what would be the fun in that?"

Once Maria is settled, I hand her two toast-and-jam sandwiches. She sets the canteen on the hood of the car, the toast-and-jam sandwiches on her lap. I slide onto the hood beside her.

And as we're just about to dig into our sandwiches, we hear our first offering.

"Now close your eyes," I say.

"Roger that," Maria says.

"It sounds like a Volkswagen Beetle," I say, lifting my head up to the sky.

"It's a Cessna, that's for sure," Maria says.

"It's not a one-eighty-two. They're . . . I don't know, just sadder," I say. "It could be a Beechcraft, maybe. . . ."

"No way. Beechcrafts are slicker. They don't rat-a-tat—" Maria says, and then I feel her body kind of shaking next to me.

"What are you doing?"

"Open your eyes real quick," Maria says. I oblige her and turn to find her flicking and fluttering her fingers around in front of her, like a tiny little finger-man running away from something.

"Rat-a-tat-tatting," Maria says. As if this is somehow clarifying.

"Is that what rat-a-tat looks like in your head?" I ask, laughing.

"Okay. Maybe it's more of this?" she asks, waving her hands in front of her.

"That's jazz hands. You're just doing jazz hands now," I say.

"Fine. Have it your way. Also? That plane is a one-seventy-two. I knew it before the rat-a-tat thing, by the way," Maria says, picking up her canteen of tea.

"You're right . . . That's—" We both pop our eyes open just as the plane flies overhead. "That's exactly what it is."

"Kinda sounds like one of the Mescaleros," I say, my mouth full of toast and jam.

Maria nods and risks another small sip of the piping hot tea.

A buzzing, rumbling engine clatters in the distance. Maria and I both close our eyes.

"That's not American," Maria says.

"No, it's . . ." The plane gets closer.

"Twin engine," Maria says.

"Italian, maybe," I add.

"You can't possibly know that," Maria says, laughing.

"I know it's Italian because that plane is a Partenavia P-Sixty-Eight, thank you very much," I say, opening my eyes.

The Partenavia soars overhead just as I take a giant, only slightly smug, bite of my toast-and-jam sandwich.

"I need to up my game if I plan on giving you a run for your money anytime soon," Maria says, arching an eyebrow.

"I mean, no rush, right? We've got . . ." I trail off.

"Forever," she finishes. I nod.

"Forever," I say. Maria gives me a nudge, and I know she's thinking it.

"Go ahead. I know it's killing you," I say.

"So cheesy," she says, laughing.

"So cheesy," I repeat.

The skies are silent for a few moments, and then I hear it. The plane's low growl in the pit of my stomach, coming closer overhead, and then closer still.

"It's—" Maria says, but then cuts herself off as we lift our faces to the sky, eyes wide open.

The engine's singsongy hum snakes up my spine, its purr both magnetic and menacing. And the most beautiful thing I've ever heard.

As *Mr. Goodnight* soars overhead, Maria and I wave and yell, hoping Jack and Bonnie can hear us.

And I swear I can hear an air horn in the distance.